AMAZING GRACE

JOHN G. HARTNESS

For Jamie —
— Find your Grace —

DEDICATION

Dedicated to the Western York County Grapevine: Faye Russell, Helen "Tot" Good, and my mother, Frances Hartness.

PROLOGUE

When I was a little girl, my best friend was named Tina. I met her the summer after my fourth-grade year, and we played together all summer long in the woods behind my house. I didn't have many friends, so when I started telling my mother about Tina, she was thrilled. I'd finally found a girl my own age to be friends with. I suppose she thought this would make school easier in the fall. I didn't believe that; I just thought it might give me a nice summer before I had to go back to school, where the girls teased me about my clothes and asked me why I always wore boys' shoes and why my clothes were old and frayed at the hems.

Tina never asked questions, just played Star Wars on our swing set Millennium Falcon and always let me be Princess Leia and never made me be Chewbacca because I was "dirty" and "smelled like a Wookie." Tina was always there that summer, just hanging around outside whenever I got done with breakfast in the morning, ready to play. She never came into my house, not even for afternoon snack, and I never went to hers. We just played together, exploring the woods and the creek and the red clay banks and getting the mud between our toes and making mudpies and taking off our blue jeans and sitting on the wet rocks in the creek in our underwear, pretending we had on bikinis like the older girls we saw on TV.

Until one morning Tina wasn't there. I hopped down the cinderblock steps at the back door of our trailer and looked around, but she wasn't nowhere to be seen. I wandered around my back yard for a little while, swung on the swing for a bit, but she didn't show up. So I went to look for her. She wasn't down by the creek, not even in the deep pool where we liked to catch crawdaddies. She wasn't in Old Man Perkins's field seeing how far she could fling cowpies before they broke. She wasn't in the old barn across the road at Aunt Hazel's place, with all its smells of hay and old horses.

Finally, I found her all the way down at the old Martin place, sitting all by herself on the steps. There weren't no house there no more, it having burned up a long time before I was born, so there was just a concrete slab foundation poured with three brick steps leading up to it, and a chimney sticking up like a red brick finger pointing at the sky.

"What you doing sitting out here all alone?" I hollered as soon as I saw her. She was still tiny off in the distance, and when she didn't say nothing, I figured she didn't hear me. I ran down the overgrown gravel driveway, thistles and grass seeds catching all up in my white tube socks I had to wear on account of the hand-me-down boots Mama got me from the church was still a little big. She allowed as how I'd grow into them by the time school started.

I was out of breath from running up that whole long driveway, so I leaned over and put my hands on my knees like I seen people do on TV when they were tired. It didn't make me feel no better, so I just sat down on the top step next to Tina.

"What you doing all the way out here?" I asked again, panting a little. Tina never got out of breath, no matter how far we ran or roamed. She could run for days if she needed to. Me, I had a little belly from watching too much TV, so Mama liked that I spent all day running around outside with Tina. She said all the fresh air was good for me. I thought she liked it that I was out of the house for her to watch her stories.

Tina didn't answer me for a long time, then she finally said, "I'm waiting for my mama." I hadn't never met Tina's mama, not in all the time we'd been playing together. I hadn't never been to her house, neither. She'd always just showed up outside in my back yard, ready to play.

"Okay, I'll sit with you. Is she gonna bring you lunch?" Tina shook her head and didn't say nothing. I just sat there with her, quiet. Sometimes she was like that, quiet and still. Other times she was just like a normal girl, least as much as I could tell, not really having any other friends to speak of.

We waited for a long time, but nobody came. After a while, I got bored and started to look around the old burnt down house. I'd been there before, a couple of times, but I always got scared and left before I could see anything. Kids on the school bus would point at this place, nothing visible from the road but the chimney, and say somebody died in the fire and that it was haunted. I wasn't scared of ghosts, not as long as Tina was with me and it was daylight.

I found a nickel and a Bible that you could still read some of the pages in, then I was rooting around in a back room and found a golden locket. The chain was melted away, but the locket itself looked like it had been under something when the fire happened, so it wasn't hurt too bad. I couldn't get it open, not even with my pocketknife. I messed with it for a long time, then turned to Tina to see if she could open it.

Tina was standing at the top of the steps with a pretty woman with long dark hair and eyes that hadn't smiled in a month of Sundays. I don't know how I knew, but I could tell that I'd never seen anyone so sad. She wasn't dressed to be outside, wearing slippers and a housecoat over her pale green nightgown, but she didn't seem to care, and I wasn't going to tell a grown-up how they should or shouldn't dress.

I walked over to them and stuck my hand out. "Hey there," I said. "You must be Tina's mama. I'm Lila Grace Carter, and I appreciate you letting Tina come play with me. She has been a good friend to me this summer."

She knelt down in front of me, putting herself eye-to-eye with me, and smiled. It was a winsome thing, a little flutter of a smile that might run away if you looked at it too hard, so I tried to pretend like I couldn't tell she didn't have many smiles in her life. "Why, thank you, Lila Grace. I appreciate you keeping my baby company these past months 'til I could come be with her again. I expect we've got to move along now, but know that wherever you go, Tina will always be your friend."

Then she stood up, motioned Tina over to her side, took her hand, and they were gone. That's all it was. One second they were standing in front of me; the next they were gone. I turned around in circles and ran around that burnt-up homestead looking and hollering for Tina, but she was gone. After what felt like hours of looking, I decided she was gone for good and trudged on home.

Mama was standing at the sink peeling potatoes for supper when she saw me walk up the driveway. "Lila Grace, you leave them nasty boots on the back porch and wash up before you come in this house!" she hollered through the screen window. I took off my boots and turned on the spigot by the back door, then let the water run through the hose for a minute 'til it got cold and washed the dirt and soot off my hands and feet and face. I dried off with an old towel hanging by the back door that Daddy used to clean up with before he came in from the sawmill at night, and I carried my boots in and set them on the porch before I hopped up to the kitchen table for some lunch. We never ate in the dining room except on special occasions.

Mama brought me a glass of sweet tea and a tomato sandwich, and I could see on her face she'd been crying. "What's wrong, Mama?" I asked as she sat down, washing down a big bite of home-grown tomato and mayonnaise with tea sweeter than lemonade.

"A woman from our church passed this morning, honey, and the whole thing made me a little sad. I was glad when you came home for lunch instead of going off all day playing today."

"Who was it?" I asked, taking another too-big bite of sandwich. Mama smiled at me as the tomato juice ran down my chin. She picked up a paper napkin off the table and wiped my face for me. I grimaced a little, I wasn't a little kid anymore, but she was upset, so I let her do it without fussing.

"I don't think you knew her, but it was Clara Good. Her family lived down the road a piece before you were born. Her husband and daughter were killed in a house fire years ago, and poor Clara never was right after that. She couldn't keep a job, and finally they had to put her in a home up in Rock Hill. Well, she died today, and it all reminded me of how sad the whole story was."

"She lived in that old burnt-out house on the other side of Mr. Sam Junior's place?" I asked, slipping the locket deep into the front pocket of my jeans.

"Yes, that was the place. You know it?"

"Only that some kids on the school bus say it's haunted." I had never lied to my mother before, but something told me that no good would come of telling her where I had spent my morning.

"She had a daughter about your age. I can't remember her name..." I watched my mother's eyes go wide, then she looked at me. I looked back at her, ready to tell her everything if she asked, or to tell her nothing. It was the first time I remember us talking like that, having a whole conversation without speaking a word, but it certainly wasn't the last time it happened.

"Finish your sandwich, sweetie. Then I need you to help me hang up the laundry this afternoon." She got up from the table, shuffled over to the sink, suddenly older than I'd ever seen her, and went back to washing and peeling potatoes. I finished my sandwich and carried my paper plate to the trash can on the back porch. While I stood there, out of Mama's sight for the time being, I pulled the locket out of my pocket. It popped right open, and I looked down at Tina's face staring into her mama's, both of them smiling like there was no tomorrow.

I closed the little golden oval and slipped it back into my pants pocket. I looked out the back door and thought for a minute that I could see a woman walking away from my house holding hands with a little girl, but in a blink, they were gone.

"Bye, Tina," I whispered, and went inside to help Mama with chores. That was the day I realized how different I really was.

CHAPTER 1

"So, you're a medium?" the large man asked me in the tone of voice usually reserved for the mentally ill or the tragically stupid. I wasn't sure which one he thought I was, but I had a pretty good guess. "That means you talk to dead people?"

"Sheriff Dunleavy," I replied, working very hard to keep a civil tongue in my mouth and remember that my mama raised me to be a lady. "I'm Southern. We all talk to dead people down here. As a matter of fact, I don't believe I can truly trust anybody that doesn't speak to at least two or three dead relations on a daily basis. The difference is, they talk back to me."

Jeff Mitchum, one of the deputies, piped up. "She's right, Sheriff. Miss Lila Grace can find things you thought was lost forever, and tell you if your wife is fooling around on you, and all sorts of things she ought not to know."

I sighed a little bit. I knew Jeff was trying to help, but he never was the sharpest knife in the drawer, and I could tell from the look on Sheriff Dunleavy's mustached face that Jeff's endorsement had most of the opposite effect the poor deputy was hoping for.

"Thank you, Jeff," I said, setting my purse down in the one chair in the waiting area of the Union County Sheriff's Department. I stepped up to the counter, resting my elbows on the chipped and stained Formica surface. "Jeffrey, darling, it is powerful hot out there today. Would you be a dear and get me a glass of ice water?" I pulled a Kleenex out from the sleeve where I had it tucked away and dabbed at my forehead.

"Yes, ma'am," Jeff said, hopping up from his ancient rolling chair and walking back behind the four desks that made up the "bullpen" of the sheriff's office.

Sheriff Dunleavy remained exactly where he had been since I stepped into the building, leaning on the frame of his office door, one eyebrow climbing to where his hairline probably used to be. "I can't get Mitchum to move that fast when a call comes in, much less to run fetch me stuff. Maybe you do have superpowers." He gave me one of those little half-smiles men get when they think they're being clever.

"Maybe I taught that child Sunday School every week for six years and brought him up to respect his elders," I replied with an arched eyebrow of my own. We stood there for a minute, staring, neither one of us saying a word, 'til finally Dunleavy cracked.

"Well, what is it?" he asked.

"What is what, Sheriff?"

"What do you want, Ms. Carter? I have a department to run, in case you haven't noticed."

"Oh, I noticed, all right, Sheriff. I noticed all the people clamoring for attention for their complaints." I gestured at the empty waiting room. "I noticed all those cars in the parking lot." I pointed out the glass door where three police cruisers and my well-loved 1986 GMC Sierra pickup sat alone in a parking lot built for thirty or more. "And I certainly noticed the preponderance of victims you are consoling right there in your very office."

I never blinked. I just looked at him. After a minute or so, Jeffrey returned with my ice water. "Thank you, Jeffrey. I appreciate that. Now, may I come in, Sheriff, or are you going to stand there and be stubborn while my talent and news go to waste?"

Dunleavy sighed a huge sigh. But I suspected everything this man did was huge. He stood a little over six feet tall and was a fit man, rare in law enforcement down here. Too much rich food and front porch sitting for a man to keep himself trim much past twenty years old.

"Please come in, Mrs. Carter," he said, walking ahead of me into his office. I followed him into his office, which was almost completely unchanged from how it looked when Dunleavy's predecessor, Sheriff Johnny Thomas held court in the room. The pictures on the wall were different, shots of Dunleavy in a tailored suit shaking hands with various smiling important-looking people from his last job, Milwaukee if I recalled correctly. A light dusting of Sheriff Johnny's cigar smoke still coated everything else, especially the padded high-back rolling chair behind the desk and the surface of the desk itself. The computer was new, one of those big all-in-one jobs, and looked out of place in the cramped room, like a spaceship in a Sam Spade novel. I ran my fingers across the top of the monitor and took my seat in the wooden visitor's chair nearest the desk.

Like most people who had been in the office more than once, I knew that the chair on the left was for normal people, and the chair on the right was the "lawyer chair." Sheriff Johnny had his brother Red take the other visitor chair out one afternoon and shave a quarter-inch off one of the front legs so it never would sit quite right. Sheriff Johnny never had much tolerance for lawyers. But the sheriff was gone now, succumbed to a heart attack in the middle of umpiring a softball game between the Baptists and the Methodists back in the spring. "Gone" of course is a relative term for me, since I saw Johnny clear as day standing in the corner of the office staring down at the newest occupant of his desk.

"Now, Mrs. Carter—" Sheriff Dunleavy began, but I cut him off.

"Ms.," I corrected.

"Excuse me?"

"Ms.," I repeated. "I am not, nor have I ever been, married. And while I appreciate the flattery inherent in the idea, it has been some number of years since I felt reasonable answering to 'miss.' Therefore, please call me 'Ms.' Or Lila Grace, if you tend toward the informal. I assure you I do not find the use of my given name offensive."

"Okay then, Lila Grace, what can I do for you today?"

"I mostly wanted to call on you to introduce myself and determine to what degree we can work together."

"Work together?" There went that eyebrow racing skyward again.

"Jeffrey explained to you that I was of some assistance to your predecessor on more than one occasion. I would hope to be able to continue that relationship with you."

"You want to work with the police department?"

"Not work with, per se. I would simply like to be able to bring you information from time to time and know that it will be treated with respect and not dismissed out of hand because of where it came from."

"And where does your information come from, Ms. Carter?"

"From the dead, Sheriff. I thought we had covered that. I am a medium. I converse with the spirits of those who have passed on. They tell me things. Sometimes I need to pass those things along to you. I need to know whether or not you will believe what I tell you, or if I will need to pursue other avenues to satisfy the spirits."

Sheriff Dunleavy's eyes went cold, and he leaned forward in his chair, putting his elbows on the desk. I thought for a moment I saw a hint of an old tattoo poking out from under his short sleeve dress shirt, but I couldn't be sure. Maybe the tip of an anchor? Was our new sheriff a Navy man? Rural South Carolina typically produced more Army men and Marines. Not many of our boys on boats.

His stern voice brought me out of my reverie. "Ms. Carter, I don't know what kind of relationship you had with Sheriff Thomas, but this is my office now, and we will run things by the book. I will take any information you bring to me seriously, and I will investigate every lead in every case, but I will not have a civilian going around town on her own sticking her nose into police business. Are we clear?"

I looked up into the corner where Sheriff Johnny stood with his arms across his chest. He was grinning fit to beat the band, and I chuckled a little. I tried to hold it in, but I couldn't.

Sheriff Dunleavy's face and forehead flashed red, and I saw a little bead of sweat pop out at his temple. "Is something funny, Ms. Carter?"

"I'm sorry, Sheriff. It's just that Sheriff Johnny is standing over in the corner behind you laughing his dead fool butt off."

"What?" Dunleavy's head whirled around; then he turned back to me, scowling.

"I'm sorry, but he's there. He's amused because this is very much like the first time I sat in this office and talked to him about a murder. He yelled at me, called me a crazy person, and told me if I ever stuck my nose back in police business that he would have me arrested and shipped off to Bull Street for a psych evaluation." I pointed at the corner where Sheriff Johnny was standing.

"So, he's in the corner of my office, just hanging out? What does he want?"

"I don't know. I haven't asked him yet. I figured since it's your office now, I should deal with the current occupant before trying to communicate with any prior tenants that might be lingering past their expiration date, if you will."

"Well, ask him," Sheriff Dunleavy said, leaning back in his chair and folding his muscular arms across his broad chest. He did cut a fine figure of a man, if a little more serious than I usually liked them. If I were a few years younger, I might have set my cap for him. As it was, I wondered if he might make a good match for Jane down at the children's desk in the library.

I turned to Sheriff Johnny and said, "What do you want, Johnny? Why aren't you back where you belong, watching soaps with Linda or doing whatever y'all do in the Great Beyond?" I'm sure Sheriff Dunleavy was disappointed that my conversing with the dead didn't seem much different than me conversing with the living, but that's how my life has always been.

Sheriff Johnny opened his mouth once or twice, but no sound came out. This happens with spirits after they've crossed over and come back—sometimes they forget how to talk. I had faith in the sheriff, though. He hadn't been dead more than four or five months. He should still be able to converse relatively easily.

"Go on, Johnny, spit it out. We ain't got all day, now."

Johnny opened and closed his mouth a couple of times, looking like nothing more than a sunfish laying on the banks of a pond after it's been pulled in. I reckon he was gonna be one of the ones that couldn't talk, after all. After a couple more tries, he just shook his head and walked up to the desk. He pointed to the middle of the desk, then made some gestures like there was something under the middle of it. Then he turned around and walked out through the back wall of the room.

"Wait, Johnny, I don't know what you're trying to tell me!" I stood up and hollered as the ghost vanished. "Dammit. Excuse me," I said as I sat back down.

"What happened?" the sheriff asked.

"I don't rightly know," I grumbled. I reached down to the floor and picked up my purse. I stood up and extended my hand. "I'm sorry to have wasted your time, Sheriff Dunleavy. It's obvious that you don't believe in my gift, so I will take my leave."

The sheriff stayed seated. "What happened, Ms. Carter?"

"I don't know, Sheriff. That's what's so damn frustrating about dealing with dead people. They tell you half what you need to know, then wander off and go back to being dead. It's worse than dating, I swear to God."

"What did he do?" Sheriff Dunleavy's voice was calm, but he was working to keep it that way. I could tell by the way his knuckles went white around the arm of his chair.

"He kept pointing to the middle of your desk, like there was something under there he wanted you to know about, but he's apparently not one of the spirits that can still talk, so it was a little hard to understand him," I replied.

"Sonofabitch!" Dunleavy sat up straight, then dropped out of his chair onto one knee and yanked out the center drawer of his desk. I sat back down in my chair as he felt around the bottom of the drawer, then got down on his hands and knees and vanished behind his desk. He emerged a moment later with a brown envelope clutched in his fist. "Got it!"

He sat back in his chair and ripped open the top of the envelope. A small brass key fell out onto his calendar desk blotter, and he pounced on it like a kitten playing with a junebug.

"What's that, Sheriff?"

"This is the key to Sheriff Thomas's file cabinet, Ms. Carter. He had one copy on him when he..."

"Died is the word you're looking for, Sheriff. Remember, I still get to talk to people after they die, so it's not quite the hardship for me that it is for most people."

"Yes, well, he had one copy on him when he died, but those keys were lost after the autopsy. And I've had no access to any old case files, or even his current case files, since I got here last week."

"Until now," I said.

"Until now," he agreed.

"When the sheriff's ghost told me where to find it."

"When you used some resources unavailable to most people to assist me in finding it," the sheriff agreed, nodding in unison with me.

"So we have an understanding?" I asked, standing and holding out my hand.

Sheriff Dunleavy stood up and shook my hand. "Ms. Carter, I'm not sure what we've got, but I'm pretty sure I'll never understand a minute of it."

CHAPTER 2

It took a week and a half, but I soon found out just how right Sheriff Dunleavy was. I was bringing in tomatoes when I first saw the poor dear, sitting on the steps to my back porch with her head in her hands. Not literally, of course. Even the dead have some sense of propriety.

I walked past her at first, giving her a glance to make sure she was really dead and not just some misguided cheerleader from the high school selling candy for the prom, or magazine subscriptions for the winter formal, or seed packets for the study abroad program. I've disappointed so many of those children for so many years, it's almost like a game now. They come up with new and even more interesting ways to get me to part with my money, and I come up with different ways to say "no." But no, this wasn't a living child here to be disappointed by an old woman on a fixed income. This child was dead; all her disappointments were now behind her.

I laid out the tomatoes on top of the washing machine on a dishtowel I'd put down that morning just for that reason and went into the kitchen. I washed my hands and face, put my gardening gloves on the windowsill over the sink, and went back out to the porch. I sat down in the rocker my nephew Jason and his second wife gave me for Christmas one year and looked at the child sitting on my steps.

"Well, come on, sweetie. Let's have it. What's got you coming to see the crazy old woman that talks to dead people? Except you being dead, that is?"

The girl spun around on the step and stared at me, her mouth hanging open. I laughed so hard I almost spilled tea all over myself, but managed to get myself together before I really made a mess. "Oh my good Lord," I said. "If you could see the look on your face, child! If you was still alive, I'd tell you to close that thing before flies got in it, but I reckon that ain't much of a problem now, is it?"

"Y-you can see me?" the child asked. "You can hear me?"

"Of course I can see and hear you, sweetheart. Ain't that the whole reason you and your little girlfriends toilet papered my front yard two Halloweens ago?" It wasn't the first time I'd seen a ghost blush, but it was still a rare enough occurrence to make me grin.

"I'm sorry about that. We didn't think about…"

"About how hard it would be for an old woman to get all that toilet paper out of the trees and the grass? Of course you didn't. That's what being a teenager is all about. And don't think you invented anything new, honey. I've been getting TP'd on Halloween since your mama was a youngin. It's a lot easier to take care of than you think. You just take a lighter to it, it burns right out before any part of the tree catches, easy-peasy. Now, what brings you to my front porch looking all distraught? And who are you, firstly? Ever since I quit teaching Sunday School at the A.R.P. Church, I don't know as many of you young people as I used to."

"We're Baptists anyway," the girl said.

"Well, I forgive you," I replied. The poor child looked terribly confused, which just made me laugh again, which just made her look even more confused. "Anyway, honey, you were going to tell me who you were?" I prodded.

"My name's Jenny Miller, and I reckon you can see I'm dead."

"I noticed that first thing. How did you die and how long ago?"

"About three days ago, I guess. Time is strange now, and I don't have to sleep, so it's a little odd. But they had my funeral today, and I think it was a Friday when I died, so it feels like about three days."

"Well, let me go get the paper, and we can see if you're in the obituaries. That can tell us quite a bit." I went into the house and pulled out the last three days' worth of *The Herald* and carried them out to the porch.

I opened the first newspaper, Saturday's edition with high school football on the front page, and a big picture of a smiling blond girl on the back page of Section A. I compared the photo with the ghost on my steps, and sure enough, it was a match. "Yes, honey, you died on Friday night after cheering our Bulldogs to a victory over Dorman in overtime. It says here that you fell down the stairs in your house and broke your neck. But I suppose that isn't what happened, was it?"

The pretty blond ghost looked up at me, her eyes brimming. "No, ma'am. I didn't fall. I was pushed. Somebody pushed me down the stairs and broke my neck, and now I'm stuck here until I get justice!" Her words built and built on each other until she was almost shouting. I felt the power roll off of her, full of anger and pain. I knew if I didn't find a way to send her to her rest, she could turn into a powerful poltergeist. This child needed to move on, and fast.

"Okay, sweetie, just calm down," I said, putting my tea down and using the same tones I used to use to calm spooked horses when I was little. "Now tell me what you remember, and we'll work from there."

"I don't remember anything," she said, her voice shaky and thready. "That's the problem. I remember leaving the game with Shelly, and then nothing."

"How did you get home?" I asked. I knew if I could get her to realize that the memories were there, that it would all work out.

"Shelly drove us. She got her license last month, and this was the first game her mom had let her drive to."

"Alright. Did Shelly come in with you, or did she drop you off in the driveway?"

"Neither one. She just stopped on the street in front of my house, and I got out. I walked up the steps to the front porch, unlocked the front door, turned around to wave goodnight to Shelly, and went inside."

"Then what?" I kept my voice low, not wanting to break her out of the almost-trance she had slipped into as she walked back through the night in her memory.

"I reached over to turn on the lights, but nothing happened. I remember thinking that was strange because the porch light was working fine, but then I remembered Daddy had installed one of them fancy battery backups on the porch light so we'd have some kind of light when the power went out. It was dark as could be, but there was a little bit of light coming in the door from the porch light, and that streetlight the power company put up in the front yard shines in through the living room window something fierce, so I could see plenty."

"What did you see, honey?" I asked.

"Nothing. I mean, nothing unusual. It just looked like my house, you know? Only dark. I went to the kitchen and got a flashlight out of the drawer beside the sink where Mama keeps all the hurricane stuff, and I went to the basement to look at the fuse box."

"Only you never made it down to the basement," I added.

"That's right," the pretty little ghost agreed. "On account of some sumbitch shoving me down the stairs as soon as I got the door open good. I remember feeling two hands on my back, then I went forward, and I remember a big flash when I hit my head...then...I'm sorry, I don't remember anything else. I woke up the next morning to the sound of my mama screaming, and I was looking down at my own body, lying there at the bottom of the stairs..." Her words trailed off into sobs, and I wanted to put my arm around her and try to give the poor child some comfort, but I knew my arm would just pass right through her. I'd done it before with other spirits, and it never went well. It just made the ghost more upset and left me feeling a little bit embarrassed.

"Okay, sweetheart, it's okay," I said in a soothing tone. "Let's go inside and have a seat while you try to think of anything else you remember from that night. You're doing real good, better than anybody would expect." I stood up, and she followed me into the house.

She stopped by the washing machine and looked at the tomatoes all spread out waiting to be washed and canned. "Did you just pick these?" she asked. "I love fresh tomatoes!" She reached out for one, but couldn't touch them. Her tomato days were over, unfortunately. She looked up at me, stricken.

"I'm sorry, honey. You can't touch things anymore."

"I know. I just forget sometimes, you know?"

I did know. I'd seen it for years with other ghosts I had dealt with. Sometimes a very powerful spirit can move things around them, but that kind of poltergeist energy is real hard to sustain, and it makes a ghost become thin and wispy, and before long, it fades away entirely. I don't know if the spirit moves on or just...fades.

That was something I didn't dwell on too much. It was more for the ladies in my Sunday School class, and I tried not to ask too many heavy theological questions around that bunch. They just let me start coming back to Sunday School about six months ago, so I didn't want to push my luck. I led the teenager's ghost into the house to see if we could come up with any other clues about her untimely demise.

CHAPTER 3

I wasn't too surprised to see Sheriff Johnny sitting in my living room when I walked in with Jenny in tow. The girl stopped, though, and when I sat down in my favorite chair, I noticed that she was still standing in the open French door frame between my dining room and den.

"Well, come on in, sweetie. He ain't gonna arrest you. Not now, anyhow." I smiled at her to let her know I was only joking and waved her into the room.

She came into the room and sat on the couch. I've never understood how ghosts can sit on furniture, but they can't turn a doorknob or handle other objects. Most of 'em can't, anyway. But for some reason, they can all sit on a chair or couch just like they still walked around breathing.

"Now, honey, let's start with what Sheriff Johnny here likes to call the real police work." I nodded to Johnny, and he smiled at me. He looked like he was only half paying attention to what we were talking about, but I knew he was listening a lot more to what me and that child said than he was listening to another *In the Heat of the Night* rerun. I mean, I like Carroll O'Conner as much as the next woman, but back-to-back episodes five days a week is a little much. But

Sheriff Johnny has got hooked on it since he showed up at my door the morning after his funeral, all mute and confused and lost.

Some ghosts can talk, some can't. I've never known what makes one of them able to communicate over another one, and it ain't like I've been dead to ask anybody. But Sheriff Johnny was one of them that couldn't speak, so he had to resort to bad sign language and gestures to get his point across. The two of us spent many an afternoon in recent months watching YouTube videos on sign language, and we got to a place where we could communicate with one another pretty good.

I reached over to the antique chest of drawers I got out of Miss Ellen Ferguson's house when she passed, and I dug around in the top drawer until I found an ink pen and a little yellow notepad. I leaned forward to Jenny and asked, "Now who do you think would want to hurt you, sweetheart?"

"I can't think of nobody, ma'am. And I mean it, too. Carla Combs was mad at me for getting homecoming queen, but she got over it when she beat me for class president. Matt Ridinger was mad at me because I beat him out for Salutatorian, but then his scholarship to Duke came through and he stopped caring about stuff around here. So, I can't think of anybody that would want to kill me."

I looked over at Johnny, who wiggled his fingers in the air for a few seconds. I nodded and turned back to Jenny. "What about any of the other girls on the cheerleading squad?" I asked. "Did any of the girls on the bottom of the pyramid want to be on the top? Or vice versa, or whatever girls get mad at each other about nowadays."

She thought for a moment, then shook her head. "No, nothing like that. I was captain of the squad, but I didn't make up any of the routines or decide anything about who got featured or anything like that. And I *was* on the bottom of the pyramid because I had strong enough legs to hold up some of those little heifers." The corner of one lip turned up a little sneer, and that was the thing I'd been waiting for —the hint of mean girl to come out.

It took me back, and not to somewhere I liked going. I went right back to seventh grade gym class and playing dodge ball. All the teams were picked except me and little Mikey Miller, who had braces on both legs and a lisp. Karen Taylor and Laura Anne Mays were arguing over who got "the gimp," and who got stuck with "Crazy Gracie," as I was called until my junior year of high school.

But Jenny's sneer was gone as soon as it came over her, and she looked up at me. "I'm sorry," she said. "I hate to call them names— that's what Miss Hope called us all. We were her little heifers, and she was our Mama Moo-Cow. I think she got picked on in school because she was a big girl." Well, I'll be. Maybe this child really was as nice as she was acting. That was going to make it even harder to figure out who wanted to kill her.

Sheriff Johnny caught my eye, and I turned to see him wiggling his fingers to beat the band. "Slow down, Johnny. You know I ain't watched them videos as many times as you have." It was true, too. Sometimes I left the sign language videos running on a loop so Johnny could practice while I went to church, or the grocery store, or just out to piddle around in my garden. He'd gotten downright good at that stuff, and when he got excited, like he was now, sometimes he was too much for me to keep up with.

He stopped, then started again. I watched his wispy hands closely, glad he wasn't too pale today for me to see all the details. Sometimes Johnny would get wispy in the middle of the day, only to grow sharper and more distinct as night fell.

I turned back to Jenny. "Sheriff Johnny was wondering if there was anybody that had a disagreement with your parents? Anybody that they argued with a bunch?"

"No, ma'am," the girl said. "I mean, they got in little squabbles with Todd Ferguson about stuff at the church, and Mama didn't shop at the farmer's market no more since she caught that Riley girl putting her thumb on the scale when she was weighing her cucumbers, but nothing to come to no fights, or nothing like that. Daddy didn't even owe nobody money, except the bank. And they ain't usually the ones to go around pushing people down steps, are they?"

"No, honey, I reckon they ain't. Bankers are usually more sneaky than that." Johnny was wiggling his fingers at me again, but I turned my head and ignored him. He hates that. Makes him madder than a frog on a frying pan to be ignored, but sometimes I had to use it like a mute button. Johnny had a bad habit of forgetting that he wasn't Sheriff no more. On account of being dead and all.

I stood up and walked to the kitchen. "You want something to drink, honey? I got sweet tea and ice water. Oh, shoot, I'm sorry." Sometimes I forget they ain't ever gonna drink nothing again, especially the ones that can talk. I fixed myself some sweet tea in an old Tupperware tumbler and walked back into the den.

"I'm sorry about that, honey," I said.

"It's okay," the girl said. "I ain't quite used to it myself, yet. Being dead, I mean." She got a pensive look on her face. "Do you know...why I'm still here? Does this mean I can't go to Heaven?" She looked like she was going to cry, the poor thing. I knew better, 'cause ghosts can't cry, but it's still a good idea to keep the supernatural visitors on as even a keel as you can manage, emotionally speaking. When a ghost loses control of their emotions, things have a bad habit of flying around the room, and I had some nice Depression Glass piece in my china cabinet that I didn't want to see get broken.

"I don't know why you're here, honey, but I've got an idea," I said. "It seems like the people who don't move on are either scared of what they're going to find when they pass from this world, or there's something unfinished keeping them here. Sheriff Johnny hangs around this old town because he ain't convinced that the new sheriff can take care of his people, so he tries to keep an eye on things. Miss Leila Dover doesn't think her husband J.R. can take care of himself without her, not realizing that he took care of himself and her the last five years when her Alzheimer's got so bad. And you got murdered, only nobody knows it, so ain't nobody looking for your killer. So, you want justice. I reckon when y'all get your outstanding issues resolved, so to speak, y'all will all move on to the land of harp music and fluffy clouds."

"Are you sure?" The child looked scared to death, which I reckon was not a real good turn of phrase for her anymore.

"I ain't sure of much, sweetie. If there's anything I've learned in my fifty-seven years on this Earth, it's that we don't know half of what we think we know, and we understand less than half of that. But I know this—if you were a good person, then you'll end up Heaven. It don't matter if you toilet papered an old lady's house on Halloween or skipped Sunday School more times than you went. It matters how you acted toward others and whether or not you are really sorry for any harm you might have caused. I am not your preacher, and I am not here to cast judgement. But if I had to guess, I would think that once we figure out who pushed you down them stairs, you can move on to the next world and see anybody that's waiting for you on the other side."

"Like my granny?" she said, smiling.

I remembered that child's grandmother the second she said it. Vera Prustley was a foot-washing Baptist, as we called them. She was as devout a woman as any I'd ever known. Didn't truck with playing cards or music on Sunday, but wasn't rude about her religion, either. I didn't know her too well, but she always had a friendly nod for me when we would pass in the grocery store, even when I was on the outs with my own church family. She had passed about six years ago, right about the time this child would have been in middle school. That's about the time when children really start to understand death and grieving, so her granny's death was something she would have carried with her.

"Yes, darling," I replied. "I think your granny is almost certainly waiting to see you again. So let's try to figure out where to go from here so you can go see Miss Vera again, and your killer can go straight to jail."

Sheriff Johnny waved his arms so wildly I turned back to him. "Yes, Johnny?"

He wiggled his fingers at me, and I gave him a little smile. "I agree, Sheriff," I said.

I turned back to Jenny. "Sheriff Johnny says your killer don't need to go to jail; we need to send his sorry behind right to Hell."

CHAPTER 4

I t ain't easy knocking on the door of a house that's grieving, especially when you know it's a child that's passed. The Miller house looked like about any other house in one of them new planned neighborhoods, called Evergreen Acres, with all the streets named after trees. Of course, not a one of the trees they named a street after is an evergreen, so the Millers lived on Maple Lane. I shook my head at how dumb some developers can be as I pulled up on the street outside their house.

There were a few cars in the driveway and on the side of the road, but not too many. It was the day after the funeral, and most of the family from out of town had already gone, leaving the poor child's mama and daddy to start trying to put their lives back together. And here I was to tear it apart again.

Reverend Aaron Turner answered the door, a scowl making his face look even more sour than usual. The Baptist preacher always looked like somebody shoved a lemon in his mouth and clamped his jaw shut, or maybe stuck that lemon someplace a little farther south. But whenever he saw me, his face scrunched up like he just took a bite of something rotten and didn't have nowhere to spit it out. I was not going to be able to talk to the parents with him in the house. I'd be surprised if I got into the house at all, given the good reverend's dim view of me and my gifts. The kindest thing he'd ever called me was a fraud, and it went decidedly downhill from there.

"Reverend," I said, so polite that butter wouldn't melt in my mouth. I held out the white Pyrex dish with blue flowers on it. "I brought a chicken pot pie. Figured these folks might be tired of broccoli and green bean casseroles by now."

"That's mighty kind of you, Ms. Carter. I'll be sure to pass it along, with your condolences, of course." He stepped back and made to close to the door on me, but he had to hold the dish with both hands, on account of the bottom being too hot for him to manage it one-handed. That made him slow getting the door closed in my face, and I pushed my way just across the threshold and held the door open with my foot.

"I don't mind coming in for a minute to pay my respects. My circle wanted me to say something to Mrs. Miller on our behalf." I wondered if it was a worse sin lying to a preacher than just lying in general because the women in my church circle group didn't have a damn thing to do with me being there and had no idea I was using their names in vain. They wouldn't have cared about that, but the lying to a preacher thing would have given Jean Dowdle a little pause, at least.

"That won't be necessary," Reverend Turner insisted through gritted teeth. The man did *not* want me in that house, particularly right then. I started to wonder if there was more to his insistence than just his general dislike for me and his completely unfounded opinion that I sold my soul to the devil.

"Who's at the door, Aaron?" The voice coming from within the house was familiar, but I couldn't put a name to it. That was odd, since I'd known most everybody in town for years.

The little bit of light coming from within the house was blotted out by the big frame of Sheriff Dunleavy stepping into the doorway between the parlor and the foyer. "Ms. Carter? How are you doing?" the sheriff asked, walking over to me, a grin splitting his face. I trusted his intentions about like I trusted a crying crocodile. A smiling lawman is never honest about his intentions. I liked my police like I liked my undertakers—solemn and grim.

"I'm fine, Sheriff. I just brought this chicken pot pie and my respects to the Millers. I heard about Jenny and just felt awful about it." I pushed past Reverend Turner and shook the sheriff's hand. "Are you here officially, or just being a sympathetic ear?"

"I'm here in an official capacity, I hate to say," Dunleavy said. "There were a couple of strange things that came up in the autopsy that I need to go over with Mr. and Mrs. Miller."

"What kind of strange things, Sheriff?" I asked. I knew it wasn't my business, and a big-city cop would never tell me squat, but I had a little hope that my hokey charm would soften Dunleavy up a touch.

No such luck. "I'm sorry, Ms. Carter. I can't comment on an ongoing investigation. I've said too much already. If you'll excuse me." He stepped past me toward the door and nodded to Turner. "Reverend."

"Sheriff." The preacher nodded back in that silent acknowledgment men do. Sheriff Dunleavy continued out the door and down the steps. I didn't see what car he got into, but it must have been his personal one. I would have noticed a police cruiser in the driveway, even if I missed Reverend Turner's big old black Lincoln Town Car with the Clergy sticker on his bumper. The man was just a little ostentatious for my tastes, with his perfectly creased pants and his big shiny car. I could tolerate fancy or judgmental, but I didn't do good when one package wrapped up both irritating traits. And Turner was fit to bursting at the seams with both.

"You need to leave, Ms. Carter. This family has been through enough without your interference and crazy stories," the preacher said in a low voice. He practically hissed at me, the bald-headed little snot. I thought, not for the first time, that Reverend Turner probably got beat up a lot in school. Not because the other children were terribly cruel, which they could be, but because he was such a little bastard.

"You're right, Reverend," I said, sugar practically dripping off my tongue. "These fine folks have lost everything that matters to them right now. I should leave them alone to their grief. My name is on the bottom of the Pyrex, so they can return it whenever they're done. But don't you go putting that dish in the refrigerator while it's still hot. It'll cool down too fast and explode."

"I know that, Lila Grace. What do you take me for, a moron?"

I didn't answer that; I just turned and left the house. After all, my mama always said if you can't say something nice about somebody, don't say nothing at all.

"What are you doing?" Jenny asked as I walked down the steps on the front porch. "Why are you leaving? Talk to me, dammit!"

I tried very hard to keep my voice low and not move my lips much as I walked to the car. There was a steady trickle of people walking up to the front door, most of them carrying Pyrex, but a few with KFC buckets and one or two even carrying grocery bags with paper plates and the like.

"I am leaving because it will not do us any good to get in a fight with a preacher on your front porch. I can come back this evening when he is leading his choir practice and have a much better chance of talking to your mama and daddy without causing a scene."

"Well, where are we going now?" she asked, fading through the passenger door of my truck and settling into the seat. She turned half around, reaching for the seatbelt, then laughed a little. "I guess I don't have to worry about seatbelts now, do I?"

"No, honey, I think you're beyond those problems. And since the only lawman in town who can see you is Sheriff Johnny, you're probably safe from getting a ticket, too. Speaking of lawmen, we're going to see Sheriff Dunleavy to ask him what was squirrelly in your autopsy. Could be he has some information that might be useful to us, and we certainly have some that he should find interesting."

I pulled the pickup out onto the street and drove around the block, then headed toward the sheriff's office. There was a familiar white Prius sitting in the sheriff's parking lot, and now I knew what Dunleavy's car looked like. I could count the number of hybrids in Union County on one hand and have a thumb to spare, so it wouldn't be any trouble seeing the sheriff coming from a mile away, even if he wasn't in his official vehicle.

I walked through the front door, wincing at the loud electronic *beeeeeep* that accompanied me. Sheriff Johnny had had a bell on a metal arm over the door, like in an old hardware store, and it was still unnerving to me the new technological sound that came with the new high-tech lawman.

"Come on in, Ms. Carter," Sheriff Dunleavy called from his office. "I didn't expect it would take you very long to get here."

"Well, then you might just be sheriff enough to take care of this county," I said. I walked into his office and paused at the door. The "lawyer chair" had been replaced, and a new chair with arms sat in its place. I sat down in the new chair, testing the soft leather. There was no wobble, and it sat just a little high, putting the occupant almost at eye level with the person sitting behind the desk. Obviously, this new sheriff didn't think he needed any help intimidating people. That in itself was a little bit intimidating.

"The old chair had one leg shorter than the other. Imagine that," the sheriff said, sitting down behind his desk. He motioned to a Styrofoam cup on the front edge of his desk. "I fixed you an ice water."

I picked up the cup and took a sip. It was very cold. "Thank you, Sheriff. You have been expecting me."

"You seem like somebody who takes an interest in things that aren't quite ordinary," he said with a mild smile.

"That sounds an awful lot like a polite way of calling me a busybody, Sheriff," I replied, fixing my own smile firmly on my face. It seemed like we were going to sit here and play the "bless your heart" game for a little while, where we made snide little comments hidden in well-mannered sentences before finally abandoning our pretenses and getting down to business.

But the sheriff had a surprise in store for me. He leaned forward, put his elbows on his desk, and stared right at me. "I've asked around about you. Seems like most everybody here believes you can do what you say you can do. Even Reverend Turner, who thinks you're in league with the devil, believes you can talk to the dead. Your own

pastor, Dr. Reese, speaks very highly of your gifts and your willing-
ness to help people. So, either you've managed to fool an entire town,
or you really do have some power to talk to dead folks."

"Like I said when we first met, Sheriff, everybody around here
talks to dead people. The only difference with me is that they talk
back." I leaned forward in my chair and looked him in the eye as
I spoke.

"Well, exactly what are the dead telling you today?" he asked.

"They're telling me that Jenny Miller didn't fall down those stairs,"
I replied.

"Do they know who killed her?"

"No, they don't."

"Then what good are they?"

"They're dead, Sheriff. They aren't Batman."

He let out a deep echoing laugh and leaned back. "I like you, Lila
Grace. Can I call you Lila Grace?"

"I wish you would, Sheriff."

"You know why I like you?"

"Because I can help you solve murders?"

"No, because you ain't scared of nothing! You have got bigger
huevos than any man I've ever met. I respect that."

"Well, that's where you're wrong, Sheriff," I said. "There's plenty of
things I'm scared of. I'm scared of spiders; they give me the willies. I'm
scared that the life I lead isn't good enough to get me to Heaven, and
when I walk up to the pearly gates, Saint Peter is going to laugh in my
face and send me down to the other place. I'm scared that I really am
crazy and just hallucinating all these dead people, and you, and
driving around town, and I'm really down in Columbia on Bull Street
tied to the bed in a pair of Depends that ain't been changed in two
days with everybody ignoring my screaming because they're tired of
listening to this old woman's mouth. I'm scared of sunspots because I
watch too much PBS. I'm scared of the government because I watch
too much C-Span. I'm scared of getting cancer from watching too
much TV, and I'm scared that I won't be smart enough, or strong
enough, or good enough to find who murdered the beautiful little girl

that's sitting in your other chair right now unable to be seen or heard by anybody in the world but me, and that she will wander this Earth forever instead of going to Heaven to see her granny again like she deserves."

I leaned back and took a drink of water. "So, there are plenty of things that scare me, Sheriff. Just none of them scare me as much as letting this little girl down."

CHAPTER 5

Sheriff Dunleavy leaned back in his chair and looked at me, one of those long, steady looks that men do when they think they're being all serious, but really all they're doing is trying to figure out what box to put you in now that you have done escaped the one they thought you were supposed to fit into all nice and neat. I've known men like him all my life, and it's better to just let them sit and "process things" and figure out what they're going to say, then go on about your business and do things the way you intended to do them in the first place, rather than getting your blood pressure up fighting them over it.

"Ms. Carter, I don't know what help you can be, but I don't have a whole lot to go on with this case, and I don't know anybody in this town, and Jeff, bless his heart, just ain't as much help as I'd like for him to be. So while I'm not sure I believe you can do everything you say you can do, I think it's gonna be a whole lot better for me to have you working with me instead of out on your own getting in my way."

"Well, Sheriff, that's certainly one way of looking at it, and since it gets me right to where I want to be, which is working on this case, I don't expect I'm going to argue with you about it. Now what can you tell me that the child hasn't been able to tell me herself?"

"I don't know what the victim has told you—"

"Jenny," I interrupted.

"Excuse me?"

"Her name is Jenny, and she is a girl. She is not 'the victim' or 'the girl' or 'the body.' She is Jenny, and I will remind you that she is still sitting right here and can hear every word. She is dead, and she is a ghost, but she is also still a little girl who is scared at what is going to happen next, and angry that she won't go to the prom, or graduate high school, or get married, or have a baby, or grandbabies, or any of the things that she was supposed to do. So, she will be treated with respect and not referred to as 'the victim.' Do we have an under-standing?" I might have slipped into my Sunday School teacher voice, the one I used on Kacey Swicegood all those years when he was trying to be distracting while I was teaching the story of the loaves and fishes.

Sheriff Dunleavy looked appropriately chastened, although I don't know if it was because of what I said, or if I just made him remember his own mama reading him out for talking ugly when he was a child. He nodded, then went on. "Like I was saying, I don't know what Jenny has told you, but we know very little about this case. The...she came home from the football game, went down to the basement for some reason, and apparently fell down the stairs."

"You say 'for some reason,'" I said. "Does that mean the power was on when y'all found her?"

"Well, yes ma'am, when we got the call Saturday morning, the power was on, and there were no blackouts the night before that got called in, so we didn't have any reason to think the power was ever out. But that would explain her going down to the basement when there was no one else in the house."

"What about her flashlight? Did she have a flashlight with her?" I asked. Jenny nodded for me to go on, but stayed silent.

Dunleavy looked at me, then picked up a folder from his desk and took some glossy pictures out of it. He spread the crime scene photos out on the calendar Joan Green, the town's only real estate agent, give out every year and started looking through them. "I don't see a flashlight in these pictures. The basement's not the cleanest place I've ever seen, but there's not much clutter," he said.

"There it is," Jenny said, pointing to one of the pictures. "On that shelf by the freezer. That's my flashlight. But how did it get all the way over there?"

"What do you mean, sweetie?" I asked, then I saw where she was pointing. On the shelf over their big freezer, the one her daddy probably put a deer in every winter, sat a bright shiny flashlight, without a speck of dust on it. I could see in the photo how much it stood out on the shelf.

"Sheriff," I said. "Jenny said that's the flashlight she was carrying when she went down the steps," I said. "We need to find out who moved it."

"Yep, because if she had it in her hand when she was pushed, somehow I doubt it flew ten feet across the basement and just happened to land perfectly on that shelf," Dunleavy agreed. "I'll get Jeff to go over there and bag it; then we can bring it back over here and dust it for prints."

"You might want to have him dust the fuse box while he's over there," I suggested.

"That makes sense. If Jenny's telling you the power was out…"

"What's the matter, Sheriff?" I asked.

"I'm talking like I believe this is all really happening, which I reckon I do, since I'm sending a deputy over to re-open a crime scene based on either the say-so of a ghost, or the say-so of a crazy woman. It's just going to take me a minute or two to adjust to my new reality, I think."

"Welcome to my world, Sheriff. Don't worry, there's plenty of room on the crazy train."

"Lila Grace, did you just make an Ozzy Osbourne reference?" Sheriff Dunleavy asked me.

"I'm hardcore, Sheriff," I replied. "Didn't they tell you I worship the devil and bite the heads off live bats?"

"Oh, people tried to warn me, alright, but believe me, their warnings could not hold a candle to the reality," he said.

"I'm so glad I could help," I said with a smile, then returned my attention to the crime scene photos. Sheriff Dunleavy called Jeff on the radio while I perused the photos and sent him over to the Miller house to collect the flashlight and dust the fuse box. He also instructed the young officer to take pictures of the stairs, regardless of the fact that a dozen people had trooped through there in the days since Jenny's death.

The scene in the photos was pretty normal for a basement, even as peculiar as a house with a basement was for Lockhart, South Carolina. The only reason I could think they would have it is the slope the house sat on made for a whole lot of usable space along the back of the house, so somebody put walls around it and called it a basement. There were some shelves with the kind of junk people usually put on their garage or crawlspace—old sports equipment, lawn furniture that's out of season or too worn out for use except when the in-laws come over and every single chair that can come out into the yard already has a behind in it, some old cans of paint, a seed spreader, a wheelbarrow with a flat tire, and a dead teenage girl.

Jenny stood looking over my shoulder, silent after telling us about the flashlight. I didn't say anything to the child, just let her look. Sometimes the dead need to see themselves lying there to really understand their new place in the world, or lack thereof. I looked up at the girl, and her face was sad, but determined.

"Are you alright, sweetie?" I asked after a minute.

"I'm fine. It just took me a minute to get my head wrapped around the fact that was me laying there. Did my mama or my daddy find me?"

I looked at Sheriff Dunleavy, then when he didn't answer, I remembered that he couldn't hear the girl. "Who found her, Sheriff? Was it her mother or her father?"

The sheriff opened another manila folder on his desk and pulled out a pink sheet of a multi-part form. "It says here that the father discovered the...found her." He caught himself before he called her "the body," and I appreciated it.

"That's good," Jenny said. "Mama wouldn't have been able to

handle that. I mean, I'm sure it was bad for Daddy, too. But Mama would have just been tore all to pieces."

"I'm sure she was that anyhow, darling," I said. "A parent ain't supposed to have to bury their child. It's about the worst thing I can imagine."

"You never had any kids, did you Ms. Carter?" Jenny asked, all of the melancholy of death forgotten in the irrepressible curiosity of the teenager.

"No, honey, I never married. I guess children just weren't in the cards for me," I said. I pushed all thoughts of a young man with glasses and a trim beard driving out of town in a fast car to the back of my head. This was not the time to dwell on old hurts or regrets. This was the time to find out who pushed that child down a flight of stairs.

"I can't see anything out of place or unusual, Jenny," I said, motioning to the pictures. "Can you?"

She leaned in closer, her body passing through my shoulder. I felt all the hair on my right arm stand up in goosebumps at her touch, like a goose didn't just walk over my grave, but stopped and decided to tap dance on it for a little while. After several long seconds, she straightened up, and I rubbed some warmth back into my arm.

"No ma'am, I don't see anything different. I didn't spend a whole lot of time in the basement, though, so I might not know it if I saw it." She looked disappointed, like she had been hoping the killer wrote his name in the dust at her feet or something.

"She didn't see anything else out of place, Sheriff," I reported. "What else do you have that we can look at?"

"I don't have any more photos, unless you want to look at the autopsy?" He looked from my face to over my right shoulder, where Jenny stood. I thought for a moment that the good sheriff could see her, then I remembered that I looked up at her whenever I talked to her, so he could easily figure out where she was from watching me.

"I don't think that will be necessary," I said. I had no interest in seeing pictures of this sweet child all cut up, and wouldn't be able to get any information that way anyway. I was no kind of doctor. All I'd get from seeing pictures of an autopsy would be nauseated.

"Good," Sheriff Dunleavy said. "The findings were consistent with a fall down the steps, but the coroner was surprised to see that there were no bruises on the knees or hands. That made him think that she might have been pushed, because a person falling would naturally put their hands out to break their fall."

"And most people who fall down the steps don't land on their head," I said.

"That's right," the sheriff agreed. "If it had been a normal fall, her legs and the rest of her would have been all bruised up. She wasn't, just her head and a broken neck. Then when I saw you at the scene, I knew life was about to get a whole lot more complicated."

"I am sorry about that, Sheriff. I would very much like for your life to be as simple as possible. Because when your life is simple, it means that my life is boring. And I like a boring life. I like to go to church on Sunday and on Wednesday nights. I like to go to the farmer's market on Saturday and buy my vegetables. I like to read the newspaper every morning while I eat my oatmeal with strawberries cut up in it and just a little bit of brown sugar to make me feel decadent. I like boring, Sheriff. So, I truly am sorry that I am complicating your life, but this poor child showed up on my doorstep crying her poor dead eyes out, and I couldn't very well turn her away."

"No, I reckon you couldn't, at that. Well, right now I've got Jeff going out to pick up the flashlight, so do you have any supernatural advice as to our next step?"

I didn't get the chance to answer because as soon as I opened my mouth to speak, the woman who was painting her nails at the reception desk when we walked by rushed in, her mouth open wide. "Sheriff, you got to come quick," she panted.

"What's wrong, Ethel?" the sheriff asked.

"We just got a 911 call come in. There's another dead girl."

CHAPTER 6

I followed the sheriff in my truck, but the closer we got to the scene, the more my heart just sank further down toward my toes. I wasn't sure when we turned off onto Highway 9 out of town exactly where we were going, but the second we turned left onto Black Bottom Road, I felt sick to my stomach.

"This is where she did it, ain't it?" Jenny asked.

"Yes, honey, this is where she did it," I replied, thinking back to that summer when Union County got famous for the ugliest of reasons. A few minutes later, we pulled up to the boat landing at John D. Long Lake, where Susan Smith rolled her car into the lake with her two children strapped in, drowning them both. I hadn't been to the lake since the day they pulled the car out, for fear of what I would see when I did, but here I was now.

"That's just awful," Jenny said.

"Yes, it is."

"Are the little boys here?" she asked.

"I hope not," I said. "I hope they went to Heaven to play and be little boys forever and have all the ice cream they want and never get skinned knees or stung by yellowjackets."

"That would be nice," Jenny said. "I hope that, too." I could feel her look at me. "You ain't been out here, have you?"

"No, I haven't. I don't know if I can do anything for those boys if they are here, and I don't know if I can stand it if I can't."

"You want me to look around and see if they're here?"

"You're sweet," I said, putting the truck in park and unfastening my seatbelt. "But I'll be fine. If there's a couple little boys out there, I reckon I'll try to help them move on. If not, then that'll be better, I think. But they aren't why we're here."

"I wonder who it is?" she asked, passing through the door to walk beside me.

There was a wrecker and an ambulance parked at the landing, and Sheriff Dunleavy was talking to Clyde, the county wrecker driver. A pontoon boat floated out in the lake, and I saw bubbles popping up to the surface around the boat. My best guess was they had Allan West down there looking around, since he was the only person in this part of the world with SCUBA gear that used it more than once a year.

I walked up to the sheriff's side. Clyde tipped his hat to me. "Lila Grace," he said.

"How are you, Clyde?"

"Oh, I been better, I been worse. Ain't looking forward to this mess."

"Why's that?"

"Cars get heavier than hell when you fill 'em up with water," Clyde said. "I ain't got but a five-ton winch on this old girl. Too much water in whatever's under there, I might not be able to pull it out. I can handle most cars, but we get something like one of them big stupid SUVs and we better be sure to break out all the windows before it comes up. That'll let the water run out easier and give me less problem winching it up onto the landing."

"What happened here, Sheriff?" I asked.

"You need to go on back outside the yellow tape, Ms. Carter." Jeff came up to me and took hold of my arm. I shook him off and gave Dunleavy a look.

"It's okay, Jeff. She's helping us on the Miller case. She can stay."

"But she's not a deputy. It's only supposed to be emergency personnel behind the tape, Sheriff," Jeff protested.

"Jeff, I get to let anybody on this side of that yellow piece of string that I want to," the sheriff said. "If it'll make you feel better, when we get back to the station, I'll deputize Ms. Carter. But for now, leave her alone and go make sure that Cracker fellow stays the hell back."

The "Cracker" in question was Gene "Cracker" Graham, the owner of the local newspaper, lead reporter, and chief photographer. Life in a small town meant he wore a lot of hats. I recognized his car pulling up to park next to my truck, and Jeff hurried off to intercept him.

"You were telling me what happened?" I asked.

"Shorty Horton was fishing out here when he hooked his line on something. Snapped it clean, so of course he decided that he'd finally found the one big catfish in Long Lake, and starts circling."

"Don't know why," I said. "Catfish that old and big wouldn't be fit to eat."

"Anyway," the sheriff continued. "He hit something with his outboard motor, and when he dove under to see what it was, he saw the car, with long blond hair floating out the driver's side window. He called it in, and you know the rest. Jeff was already on the scene when I got here, and he'd called Clyde. I got Allan out here, and once he gets the winch hooked up, we're going to pull it up out of there and see who the poor woman was."

"I thought Ethel said it was a girl?" I asked.

"Lila Grace, have you seen Ethel lately? Anybody who ain't drawing Social Security is a boy or a girl, including you and me."

I laughed. "Well, I think I'm a fair bit closer to getting my government check than you are, but it's still a ways off. I can't even get free sweet tea at Hardee's yet."

"I got it!" Allan shouted from across the lake.

"Get your boat out of the way and we'll pull her up," Clyde hollered back. Allan heaved himself out of the water, looking like the Michelin Man in his wetsuit. He waddled to the captain's chair, leaving a trail of fins, tanks, and mask as he went. Seconds later, the pontoon boat putt-putted off to the far side of the lake and Clyde put the winch in gear.

It whined with the load, but the old rollback wrecker had more than enough power to pull the black Honda Civic up out of the water. As soon as the back bumper crested the lake's surface, I heard Jenny gasp.

I turned to her, my eyebrows up. "What is it, sweetie?" I asked, trying not to let on to Clyde that I was talking to a ghost. He didn't believe in what I did, and didn't look too fondly on my talking to dead people around him.

"That's Shelly's car. Oh my god, it's Shelly!" The dead girl collapsed weeping to the ground, more upset about her friend's death than I'd seen her about her own.

"Sheriff," I said quietly. "We have a problem."

"What's wrong, Ms. Carter?"

"That car belongs to Jenny Miller's best friend Shelly. She was the last person to see Jenny alive, and now she's probably the drowned child in the driver's seat of that car."

"Son of a bitch," the sheriff said under his breath. "Pardon my language, Ms. Carter."

"Hell, I was just thinking the same thing myself, Sheriff," I said, splitting my focus between the car slowly rolling backward up the boat landing and the sobbing teenage ghost at my feet.

Sheriff Dunleavy motioned his deputies to push the lookie-loos farther back and went over himself to break up an argument between Deputy Jeff and the newspaperman Gene Graham, who had indeed shown up with a big old Nikon camera slung around his neck like a hillbilly Jimmy Olsen. Cracker was waving his arms and starting to wind himself up into a whole tirade about the First Amendment and freedom of the press when I walked up.

"Gene," I said, my voice cracking through the muggy air like a whip. Gene's head whipped around like he was back in my Sunday School class and I'd caught him trying to get a reflection up Renee Hardin's skirt in his patent leather dress shoes again. That boy never would believe me when I told him patent leather didn't reflect, no matter how much you polished it. He was a little scamp, but it did mean he always had polished shoes for church, so I let it go.

"Ms. Lila, what are you doing here, and on the other side of the tape, too?" Gene asked.

"The sheriff has done told you he can't answer no questions, Gene. Now you need to put that camera back in your car and go interview Arthur Black about how his peaches are coming in after the cold snap we had in April. As soon as the sheriff has something he can tell you, he'll call you and give you an exclusive." I didn't bother to point out that since he owned the only newspaper in town, he always had an exclusive. Ever since that mess with the Smith woman happened, Cracker liked to think he was a big-time newspaperman. He had one story picked up by the Associated Press, and it went straight to his head, I swear.

"Now, Ms. Lila, I can't do that. This is the biggest news to happen in Lockhart this week, and I have to cover it. I need to report on it, and I can't do that without taking some pictures."

"That is not going to happen, Mr. Graham, and if you point that camera anywhere near that vehicle without my permission, I swear on my mother's grave you'll find it at the bottom of the lake," Sheriff Dunleavy growled.

Gene bowed up again, and I could just about see these too men getting ready to whip things out and start measuring, so I leaned into Gene and whispered, "We think it's Shelly Thomas's car, but we can't have nothing getting out about it until we see if she's in there and then notify the next of kin. You wouldn't want that child's mama reading about it in the newspaper before we get a chance to break the news to her, would you?"

Gene's face went ghost-white, and he took a step back from the yellow police tape. He stood there for a minute, then took a deep breath and wiped his eyes. "No, Ms. Lila, that would be awful. I see what you mean. I can go…cover some other stories and wait for word from the sheriff that he has information. Y'all know where to find me." He turned and waddled off back to his truck and peeled out of the parking lot. I started walking back to the car, and Sheriff Dunleavy followed close behind.

"What was that all about, Ms. Carter?" he asked.

"Gene played baseball with Shelly's daddy in high school. They fell out when Shelly's daddy stole Gene's girlfriend."

"Why would that make Graham back off the story?"

"Gene's girlfriend married Shelly's daddy and had three little girls. The oldest one is about sixteen, and I'm afraid we're about to find her in the driver's seat of that car."

"So Gene doesn't want to upset his old girlfriend, I get it."

"Gene doesn't want to break the heart of the only girl he ever fell in love with, Sheriff. He never got married, never had kids. He and the Thomases became real close after they got married, and Gene is godfather to all three girls. He would no more hurt that family than he would sell his newspaper to a Yankee."

The car was all the way up on dry land now, and Clyde was lowering the end of the rollback to pull the car up onto the wrecker. Sheriff Dunleavy waved him to a stop and walked around the car. I followed close behind, looking where he looked, but I couldn't see anything out of the ordinary.

"What do you see, Sheriff?" I asked.

"Not much," he said, his eyes scanning the car as we did a slow lap around the outside. "There's nothing to indicate that she wasn't driving or operating the car under her own power when it went into the lake. We won't know more until we get it back to the garage, but all the windows are intact, and I can't see any scratch marks around the keyholes to indicate forced entry."

He paused at the driver's door, peering inside. "Is that Shelly?"

I looked in the window and nodded. Shelly Thomas was sitting up behind the wheel, pretty as you please in a cute pink top and blue jeans. Her seatbelt held her upright, and there was no air bag deployed, so it didn't look like she'd been in a wreck. I couldn't see too much through the windows, all streaked with silt and lake muck, but I couldn't see any injuries on her. She just looked like a pretty teenaged girl out for a drive.

The sheriff motioned the EMTs over to the car and snapped on a pair of latex gloves. I stepped back out of the way as they rolled a stretcher over to the side of the car and opened the door. Water poured out onto the ground, and everybody stepped back.

Clyde walked up to me with a sheet in his hands. "Take a corner, Lila Grace," he said, holding out the white fabric to me.

"What are we doing, Clyde," I asked, then a lightbulb went off as I watched him walk away from me as far as he could while we each had one corner of the sheet, and he lifted his hand above his head. I did the same, and we held that old ragged sheet up like a curtain as the EMTs and Sheriff Dunleavy got the girl out of the car and onto the stretcher. They zipped her up in a body bag and covered her with another sheet before one of them nodded to Clyde and we let the makeshift privacy screen down.

I walked over to Clyde and helped him fold the sheet. "That was sweet of you, Clyde," I said.

"People deserve not to have everybody in the world gawking at them when they're laying there dead, Lila Grace," he said. "I started carrying this in my car some fifteen years ago, when that kid ran his car into the bridge railing down on Old Pinkney Road."

"I remember that wreck," I said. I didn't bother telling Clyde that I had talked with that poor boy several times before he got satisfied enough that his mama would be fine without him and he was able to move on.

"There was a bunch of people at that one, like there is today, and that boy was all tore up. His head was about split plumb in two, and I remember thinking that it wasn't fair to him that all them people that didn't even know him were looking at him like that. So now I try to give people a little dignity in death. It's the least I can do."

"It matters more than you think, Clyde," I said.

"I reckon if anybody would know, it'd be you," he said, then turned and put the sheet in the cab of his truck. I stood there flabbergasted. I'd had a lot of people say a lot of things about my gifts before, but never had anybody just accepted them for what they were like Clyde. I swear, that little old man was a true onion. He had more layers than anybody would ever suspect.

I looked to Sheriff Dunleavy to ask him what our next move was, but caught sight of Jenny as I turned my head, and the look on her face stopped me in my tracks.

CHAPTER 7

I walked over to the ghost and tried to speak to her without it being obvious to the dozen people standing behind the police cordon just a few yards away that I was talking to empty air. It's not an easy task, but it's one that I have somewhat mastered over the years.

"What's wrong, sweetie? You look like somebody just ran over your dog." I realized as soon as the words crossed my lips that it wasn't the most polite way of talking to a dead child who just found out that her best friend is dead, too. But there aren't any instruction manuals for my kind of life, and I couldn't take it back, so I just had to roll with it.

"Where's Shelly?" Jenny asked, glowing tears rolling down her face. This was a new one on me. I'd seen ghosts angry, and sad, and even seen a couple of them scared of what was coming next, but I'd never seen one cry before. But here she was, sobbing just like you'd expect a girl whose best friend's car just got pulled out of a lake to do. Her tears weren't solid, of course, but they were part of her, a little tiny piece of Jenny's soul cascading down her cheeks, cutting little trails of faintly glowing light across her shimmering visage.

"What do you mean, where's Shelly?" I asked. I didn't want to come off as crass and say that she was on the stretcher being loaded into the back of the ambulance, where do you think she is, you idiot, but that's kinda what I was thinking.

"I don't see her. I could see Sheriff Johnny, and I've seen a couple of other ghosts as I've been walking through town since I...since we first met. But I don't see Shelly. Where is she?"

I looked around. The child had a good point. I didn't see Shelly, either. Far as I could tell, Jenny was the only ghost at John D. Long Lake, and I was powerful glad of that. I didn't relish the idea of telling Shelly that she was dead, especially if it had happened as recently as I expected it had. And worse than that, I sure didn't want to run into the poor Smith children if they happened to be lingering all these years. I didn't expect them to, not after all this time, but you never know. Some people have powerful attachments to places, and some people have powerful reasons for wanting to see justice done. None of that is normal for little kids, but there's no hard and fast rules about the afterlife.

"I don't see her, sweetie. Maybe she's not here."

"Why wouldn't she be here? Where would she be?" Jenny was starting to get more upset, and her sadness was turning to anger, which was starting to stir up the rocks and dust around her feet. I stepped back and took a look around. We hadn't drawn much attention yet—everybody was still focused on the macabre ceremony of loading poor Shelly's body into the ambulance—but that ritual was almost complete, and we would be the most interesting thing by far in a minute or so.

"Jenny, I need you to calm down," I said in my reassuring teacher voice. It's different from the steely tone I used on Cracker earlier, but it still got through to the distraught child. A couple of pebbles dropped to the ground as she stopped rocking back and forth and focused on me.

"That's good," I said, keeping my voice low and calm. "Not everybody stays around after their bodies die, not even people who are killed or have a good reason to stay. It may be that Shelly didn't have any great desire to see justice done for herself, or maybe she was just okay with moving on."

"But...then why am I still here?" She looked up at me, more tears flowing down her face. She was calmer now, but the pain in her voice was heartbreaking.

"I don't know, darlin'," I said. "I have no idea what makes one person linger and one person pass on to the other side. If I did, I'd be able to help people move on a lot faster, I think."

"Is that what you're trying to do with me? Help me move on?"

"That's the ultimate goal, isn't it?" I asked. "You don't want to stick around Lockhart dead forever, do you? I want to find out who killed you, so he or she doesn't hurt anybody else, but I also want you to be able to go to your rest."

"You mean Heaven," the girl said with the firm conviction of a Protestant teenager who's never questioned her faith for even one second.

I had no such convictions anymore, unfortunately. "I mean whatever you think I mean, honey. I think it's probably a little different for everybody, and I'm pretty sure there's not a lot of harps involved, but I know that whatever's on the other side waiting for you, it's a damn sight better than walking around talking to an old woman who's going to get locked up in a room with padded walls if she keeps standing on the boat landing talking to thin air."

Jenny smiled and sniffed. She was a cute little thing, even dead and weepy. "Thank you, Ms. Lila. I still don't know why Shelly wouldn't want to stick around and find her killer, but I reckon we can take care of that for her."

"I expect we can," I agreed. "Now let's go see if the sheriff has any ideas on how we can do that."

I walked back over to the car, where Sheriff Dunleavy had just raised the hood. I stuck my head under there beside him and said, "I think that's the engine, Sheriff."

"Thank you, Lila Grace. I'm no mechanic, but I think you're right."

"Is there anything in the engine that will tell us who killed this child?" I asked.

"Not that I can see," he replied.

"Has anything been tampered with, like on the TV shows? Brake line cut, anything like that?"

He pointed to a square thing sitting on top of another thing. "That's the master cylinder. It looks fine. I can't see where anything was tampered with there."

"Does that have anything to do with the brake lines?" I asked.

"You don't know anything about cars, do you, Lila Grace?"

"I know where the gas goes in, I know to change the oil in my truck every five thousand miles, and I know to change my tires every three years. Anything past that, I ask Clyde. His nephew Brownie runs a service station and takes care of all my automotive needs."

"Then why do you keep asking me about the brake lines?" the sheriff asked.

"On the TV shows, whenever two people poke their heads under the hood of a car that somebody died in, they always come out and say that the brake lines were cut. I just wanted to see if that happens in real life, too."

"You watch too much *NCIS*, Lila Grace."

"That may be, Sheriff, but I can't help it. That Mark Harmon is just adorable. I like the New Orleans one, too. The LA show is okay, but I don't like those actors as much. They're too pretty."

"Well, nobody cut any brake lines on this car," the sheriff said, straightening up. I followed suit, and he slammed the hood down, motioning for Clyde to load the car onto his wrecker. "In fact, as far as I can see here, the car was in perfect working order before it went into the lake."

"So why did it go into the lake?" I asked.

"Well, somebody wanted it to go into the lake. That's why they drove it in there."

"I reckon what we have to do next is find out who."

"Yeah, that's not the worst thing we have to do next." I looked at the sheriff, and his face was grim.

"Oh," I said, my voice soft. "Do you want me to go with you?"

"Do you have any particular connection with the family?"

"No," I said. "I know them, but only to speak in the grocery store. We don't go to church together, so I never had Shelly in any of my Sunday School or Vacation Bible School classes."

"Then you'd better leave this to me. I don't suppose she's..." He waved a hand around in the air.

"No, she's nowhere to be seen, Sheriff. I think she has already moved on."

"Pity," he said. "Maybe she could tell us something about the bastard that did this. Pardon my French."

"Bastard isn't French, Sheriff. *Merde* is French, and I won't bruise if you cuss around me."

"Just the same, I'll try to keep it clean. Feels like cussing in front of my mama. Just ain't natural."

"I'm pretty sure your mama knows those words, too, Sheriff."

"Oh, I can guarantee you she does. My daddy was a Marine. She's heard them all."

"Was a Marine? It was my understanding that you're always a Marine."

"He passed two years ago. That's the only way you stop being a Marine, Ms. Carter. You stop being."

"Well, I'm sorry, Sheriff. The loss of a parent is a hard thing to get over, no matter when it comes."

"I reckon the loss of a child is, too," he said. "If you'll excuse me, I'm going to go make this the worst day of a couple parents' lives."

"I'll meet you at the station in the morning, and we can talk about the fingerprints on that flashlight in Jenny's basement and look for connections between these girls' deaths." I watched him walk to his car and throw his hat on passenger seat. I did not envy the big man his duties this afternoon.

"Do you think the same person that killed me killed Shelly?" Jenny asked. I didn't hear her come up, but she only made noise if she tried to, or spoke.

"I don't think it's a coincidence that two best friends in a town of less than ten thousand people wound up dead within five days of each other. Do you?"

"No, I guess not."

"Then let's go back to your house. I need to talk to your mama and daddy. Without that son of a bitch preacher of yours looming over us."

CHAPTER 8

Thirty minutes later, I was back on the porch of the Miller house. Jenny stood next to me, and I wasn't real sure who was more nervous, her or me. I raised my hand to knock on the screen door, then put it down. I repeated the process two more times before I decided to just bite the bullet and knock.

A man in his mid-forties came to the door, well-dressed despite looking like he hadn't slept in several days. He stood on the other side of the screen in a polo shirt and khakis, the uniform of the Southern middle-class father. I heard a choked sob from Jenny, but when I glanced in her direction, she was gone. Looked like I was on my own for this one.

"Mr. Miller?"

"Yes, I'm David Miller. Can I help you?"

"Mr. Miller, I'm Lila Grace Carter. I live over on Spring Street. I... I'm working with Sheriff Dunleavy investigating your daughter's death, and I have a few questions, if you have a few minutes."

"Can this wait, Ms. Carter? This isn't a good time. My wife just learned that my daughter's best friend Shelly..." His face crumpled for an instant, but he pulled himself back together. "I'm sorry. We just got some sudden news, and my wife is very upset."

"I understand, Mr. Miller. I was just with the Sheriff," I said, wondering a little how the word got out this fast. Sheriff Dunleavy would have barely had time to go talk to Shelly's family, and the Millers already knew. Word spreads fast in small Southern towns, and never faster than when the news is awful. "But we would really like to get any information you have as soon as possible. If there's any way…"

"Okay, fine," he sighed. "But out here. My wife is…resting right now. I don't want her disturbed." He motioned to a pair of white wooden rocking chairs on the porch, an accessory that almost should come with the porch in the rural South. I took a seat, and he put his hand on the other one before stopping himself.

"I'm sorry, I'm being rude," he said. "Can I get you anything to drink? Sweet tea? Pepsi? Ice water? I think there's even some Cheerwine in there. I don't know what all people have brought, but there's at least half a dozen two-liters on the kitchen counter."

"I'm fine, Mr. Miller. Please, sit down for a minute." He sat, and we rocked while I tried to figure out where to begin.

"I know some of these questions will probably be repetitive, but with Shelly's disappearance, there might be a connection—"

"Do you think whoever hurt my Jenny took Shelly, too?" he asked. There was a flicker of hope in his eyes that I had to temper, or he wouldn't be able to focus enough to be any use to me.

"I don't know, sir. I just know that we're a small town, and a pretty safe one, usually. But here we are with two best friends falling victim to something, I don't know if it's bad luck or what, within just a few days of each other."

"It's not bad luck," Mr. Miller said. "Somebody came into this house and killed my Jenny. If that's the same person that hurt Shelly, then I reckon I'll have help when I gut the bastard. If it wasn't, then I'll get him all to myself."

I didn't have anything to say to that. I wasn't really working for the police, just working with them. A little. Begrudgingly. Plus, I pretty much agreed with him. I decided to just let it lie, rather than trying to give him some line of righteous crap about what his daughter would have wanted.

"Mr. Miller, can you think of anyone who would have wanted to hurt your daughter?" I asked, keeping my tone as gentle as I could. I'd helped Sheriff Johnny with a few cases, but I'd never talked to a grieving parent while I tried to find out who killed his child before, and I felt like I was walking on eggshells.

"No, nobody. She was a cheerleader, in the FCA, ran track, was vice-president of her class, all that stuff. She was a sweet child; everybody loved her."

"Was there anyone with a grudge, anyone that may have imagined some reason to dislike her? A classmate, and ex-boyfriend, anything like that?"

"Nothing," he insisted. "Jenny didn't date. It wasn't allowed. We let her go out in groups and some double dates with Shelly, but nothing serious."

I tried a different angle. "What about Shelly? Was she as...well-liked as Jenny?" I knew the answer I expected, and Mr. Miller didn't disappoint.

"No," he said quickly. "Shelly was a little wild. She was something of a mean girl, and I know she put down some of the less popular girls in school. Jenny was always telling us about something Shelly had pulled on an underclassman, or a girl in their gym class, or some poor child that tried out for the cheerleading squad."

"Did Jenny mention anyone specifically that Shelly was particularly rough on?" I knew that anyone with a grudge against Shelly probably didn't care much for her best friend, either. I'd also spent enough time with teenaged girls, having been one once upon a time, to know that whatever Shelly did, it was unlikely that Jenny was blameless in the affair.

"I can't think of...wait, there were a couple." The distraught father held up a finger as ideas came to him. "There was Ian Vernon, the photographer for the yearbook. Shelly hacked his phone and sent texts to all the girls in school with dirty pictures, making it look like it came from Ian."

"That's more than a little mean girl stunt, Mr. Miller. That could cause serious problems for Ian in the future." I was expecting some teasing, but not hearing that Shelly committed a felony to harass a classmate.

"I know, but you know how kids are, right?" I decided not to get into that discussion with him just days after the death of his daughter. "Was there anybody else that might hold a grudge against Shelly?"

"I guess any girl that didn't make the cheerleading squad probably hated both of the girls," he said. "Jenny and Shelly were the ones who decided on the team, with some help from Miss Hope, their advisor. Last year there were a few girls who got upset, but from what I understand, they put some new systems in place this year to make it more transparent. Score sheets and things like that, and they had individual meetings with all the girls after tryouts to tell them why they didn't make the squad and what they could work on for next year. From what Jenny said, it worked real well." I knew Debbie Hope, and that sounded like something she would do. She was a heavy girl in school, and now that she had started teaching, she was the kind of teacher that wanted everybody to feel like they were being treated fairly.

"What about boyfriends?" I asked again. "I know you said Jenny didn't date, but what about Shelly?" I found it hard to believe that two high school cheerleaders wouldn't at least go on dates.

"She had a few boys that she went out with from time to time, but nobody serious. Jenny and Shelly would go to the movies with Derek and Edward sometimes, and I think Shelly went to the prom with Tony Neefe last year."

"Who did Jenny go with?"

"She didn't go. She was supposed to go with Steven Whitaker, but he started dating a girl, and he wanted to take her instead. So, Jenny didn't go. She was just a sophomore, so she still had two proms, so she wasn't upset."

"Really? Had she bought a dress?" I remembered back in the Dark Ages when I went to prom—buying the perfect dress was more of an ordeal than trying to keep your knees together all night after the prom.

"Oh, no," her father replied. "If I'd laid out that kind of money, there would have been a whole different conversation. No, she never..." He choked up, probably thinking of all the pretty dresses he was never going to get to buy his little girl. My heart broke for the poor man, but I felt like I had to keep pressing. With two dead girls within days of each other, there had to be some connection, if we could just see it.

"I'm so sorry, Mr. Miller. But could you just—"

"What are you doing here?" I turned looked up at a pretty blond woman in her early forties standing on the other side of the screen door. She was obviously Jenny's mother—the hair, eyes, and nose were almost identical. But I'd not seen Jenny's mouth twist up into that kind of scowl, and I'd certainly not heard her speak with such venom.

"I'm sorry." I stood up and held out my hand. "I'm—"

"I know who you are, charlatan. Reverend Turner has told me all about you." Mrs. Miller spun around and disappeared into the house. I heard her footsteps stomp through the house, then I heard the sound of a refrigerator opening and closing with a *thud*.

The angry woman walked out onto the porch holding a blue and white Pyrex dish with flowers that I recognized as my own. "We didn't wash the dish because I wouldn't touch any food that came from your house. When Reverend Turner told me you came here, I couldn't believe him. I couldn't understand for a second why a heathen like you would want to set foot in the home of a God-fearing family in their time of grief. And now I come out onto my front porch and see you flirting with my husband? You need to leave, right now, and take your witchery with you."

I was stunned. Speechless. I'd been called a lot of things in my life: heathen, godless, witch, liar, fake—you name it, I've heard it. But I've never in my life had someone speak to me with the abject loathing that Karen Miller unleashed on me in her den.

I looked down, working hard to keep my temper under control. It was not an inconsiderable struggle, but I somehow managed to speak with a civil tongue. When I felt like I could speak without screaming at her, I said, "Mrs. Miller, I am so sorry for your loss, and the last thing I want to do right now is further upset you or your husband. I will go, but please understand that the police have reason to believe that Jenny may not have fallen, and now they have found Shelly Thomas's car in John D. Long Lake, so they have asked me to help with the investigation. I am not trying to do anything other than ask your husband a few questions—" I snapped my mouth shut as she held up a hand.

"Out," she ordered. "Get out and do not ever set foot on my property again. Take your dish, and your casserole, and your lies, and your devil worship and stay the hell away from my family."

I nodded. I couldn't see any way to do anything else, so I just nodded my head and turned to go. I stopped on the sidewalk and turned around, looking at the grief-stricken man sitting in the rocking chair and the fuming woman just inside the threshold. "I hope y'all can find peace. I hope that the police can find who did this terrible thing and bring them to justice. I am truly sorry for your loss."

Then I turned and walked down the sidewalk, got into my truck, and nestled the casserole dish onto the passenger side of the bench seat amongst a jacket and some other junk to keep it from sliding around. I put then the old girl in gear and pulled onto the street, making a right turn, then a left, then another right until I sat in the parking lot of the big Presbyterian church where I grew up.

I unfastened my seatbelt, leaned my head on the steering wheel, and let the tears of pain and shame and anger pour down my face. "Dammit, dammit, dammit!" I shouted in the privacy of my truck's cab. "Lord, I know I don't talk to you as often as I should, but I have to ask—why can't they just let me try to help them? Why do these people have to be so damn *mean*?"

I sat there for a couple more minutes, then pulled a pack of Kleenex out of the glove box and blew my nose. I tossed the tissue into the passenger seat floorboard and got out to walk the cemetery and talk to my people a little while.

CHAPTER 9

Walking amongst the dead always brings me peace somehow. I know it's the opposite for a lot of people, but I find the company of the resting dead awful relaxing. As much time as I spend with the restless dead, it's exceedingly peaceful to walk among those who have gone on from here.

So that's what I did. I walked along the front row of the cemetery, right there on Front Street, with my truck parked all catty-wumpus like I'd been drunk as Cooter Brown when I pulled into the parking lot. I lingered for a second in front of the three-sided monument that Cousin Bowman had collected money from everybody in the family to put up back in the 1964. My daddy gave him twenty dollars and bought four copies of the book he wrote about our family's travels across the ocean from England to the South Carolina upstate, and told Bowman to get the hell out of his face and not to never ask him for another dollar while he was trying to eat.

In defense of Daddy's manners, he said he was trying to eat some of Aunt Eller's coconut cake, and her coconut cake always was everybody's favorite. She'd make this three-layer white cake so moist if you squeezed it, you could get water for days. Eller always made Cool-Whip icing with a bunch of shaved coconut all through it, so you got some coconut in the icing between the layers of the cake, too. It wasn't like some of them store-bought coconut cakes, which is basically a white sheet cake with some coconut sprinkled on top. I tried for years to learn how to make cake like Aunt Eller, but I never could figure it out. Then she passed, and then Daddy passed, and I never married, so I didn't have anybody to teach me, nor anybody to eat it, so I just quit trying. It's probably been a twenty years since that old Tupperware cake carrier has seen any use.

I looked at that monument, tracing the Carters, and the Thomases, and the Feemsters all the way back to whatever little piece of English soil they sprang up from. The original Johnny Thomas in this part of the world was from Wales. He was old Sheriff Johnny's grandpappy with about a dozen greats in front of it. Me and Johnny always knew we were some kind of kin, but being Southern, we just called it "cousins" and let it go at that. My mama always could rattle off what number cousin you were to somebody and how many times removed, but I never got the hang of it.

I walked a little farther and took a seat on a headstone in front of my granny's stone. I was sitting on Mr. Bo Mickle's stone, and I usually made it a point to apologize to Mr. Bo for disrespecting him that way, but I'd been doing it so long by that point that I reckoned Mr. Bo would have found some way to let me know if it bothered him.

"Hey, Granny," I said. She wasn't there, of course. Granny died when I was about thirteen, and she didn't linger but a couple of days. I met her right here the morning after her funeral and watched her walk into the light. It wasn't like she walked up into the clouds like the end of *Highway to Heaven* episode, but there was a bright white light, and she told me she loved me, and told me to be good, and then she turned around and went away. So, I knew she wasn't listening in, but somehow that made it easier to talk.

"Granny, I'm having a terrible time with this one. The poor little girl wants my help so bad, but her mama and daddy won't have any of it. Her mama won't, anyhow. That preacher Turner has got his hooks into her so deep you'd think she was going to make a big donation or something. I'm sorry, that wasn't very Christian of me. But he just makes me so mad sometimes. It's like he knows I want to help people, and he keeps trying to get in my way anyhow."

I got down off the top of Mr. Bo's rock and moved over to sit cross-legged on the grass right in front of Granny's stone. I'd done this forever, but the older I got, the harder it was to get up off the grass when I was done. I reckoned it wouldn't be too many more years before I was going to have to have a cane or some kind of walking stick if I was going to go traipsing around in cemeteries. This one wasn't too bad, but some weren't maintained as good, like the one where Pap was buried.

Yeah, Granny and Pap didn't lay to rest together. They weren't even in the same town. Granny was right here in Lockhart, but Pap was way over in Chester. He remarried after Granny went, and that was about the last we saw of him. It was like he wanted nothing more than to forget our family and go be with a new one. I didn't like it, and I could tell it hurt Mama something awful, but we respected the old man's wishes and left him alone. He lived a long time after Granny passed, 'til he was well into his nineties. I only heard about it when he died because I read the obituary. There was no mention of our family in the listing of relatives. Since I wasn't family anymore, I didn't go to the visitation.

I did go to the funeral, though. I stood back away from everybody and watched them lay the old man to rest. When all the rest of the mourners got back in their cars, I walked up to the graveside and stood there for a minute watching the men lower the casket into the dirt. I was just about to walk back to my truck when he stepped up beside me.

"You still see ghosts, Lila Grace?" my dead grandfather asked me.

I nodded. I didn't really want to talk to him. I didn't know what to say. This was the man who had made me a rocking horse for Christmas when I was three years old. A rocking horse I had until I was a grown woman and gave it to a young couple at the church who had a little boy who loved to play cowboy. This was also the man who abandoned my mother when she needed a parent most, when she was burying her own mother in that ugliest cycle of life. The man that turned his back on my family for over two decades, and now stood next to me while I watched his body being lowered into the ground and tried to decipher my feelings.

"I expect you got some questions. If you'd see fit to come with me for a minute, I'd like to answer 'em."

Well, the old man knew he had me then. I was so curious when I was little that he used to call me "Cat." "Get on out of here, Little Cat," he'd say when he caught me snooping in his or Granny's closets, trying to find Christmas presents or birthday presents, or just old pictures of him from the War or of Granny when she was young woman.

None of that curiosity faded as I grew up, and getting older did nothing to tame that curious Little Cat, so I followed the old man. He walked around to the back of my truck and motioned at the tailgate. I opened the tailgate and sat down on it. He sat next to me, and this let us sit together without being forced to look at one another. I liked that arrangement.

"Best thing about driving a truck, Little Cat," he said. "You carry your car, and a table, and a seat with you all in one."

"Don't call me that," I said, my voice suddenly that of a seven-year-old girl again.

"Why not? It's what I've called you for years."

"No," I corrected. "It's what you used to call me. You ain't called me nothing in years."

"Well," he said, looking at the laces on his boots. He was dressed like I always used to see him, in a checked flannel shirt, blue jean overalls, and brown work boots. Most ghosts present wearing what they died in, but some wear what they're most comfortable in. Sometimes they'll get a look at their funeral, and all of a sudden it will switch to what they were buried in. Dickey Newton showed up one day wearing nothing at all, dead as a doornail and naked as the day he was born. I sent Dickey away and told him not to show his face, or any other part of himself, around me until he learned to manifest himself at least a pair of britches.

"What are you still doing here, Pap?"

"I stayed to see you. I'm glad you came to the funeral."

"I felt like it was the right thing to do."

"For me or for you?"

"For me. What you thought hasn't been on my mind much since you wrote us out of your new life." I could hear the bitterness in my voice, but I didn't care. He hurt my feelings when he just up and abandoned us like that, and I reckoned he could know it.

"I am sorry about that, Lila Grace."

"If you hadn't done it, I reckon you wouldn't have nothing to be sorry for."

"Well, you're right about that. It was wrong, and it was selfish."

"So why'd you do it?"

He didn't say anything for a long time, and when he finally spoke, his words were slow, like he was picking them carefully. "After your granny died, I was a mess. We had twenty-seven good years together. I guess that ain't really true. We had twenty-four good years, with enough bad days throughout to make up a year or two, and the last year was pretty rough. When your granny got sick, I didn't do nothing but take care of her for a year. It was hard on me, but that's what a husband is supposed to do.

"Well, when she was gone, I didn't have that purpose any more. I couldn't remember what it was like to be anything more than the man with the sick wife, and every time I saw your daddy, or any of my family, all I saw was her face. It didn't take long until I couldn't stand that anymore, so I left."

"You always told me that a man faces up to what's hard."

"That's true. I just wasn't much of a man right then. So I went away, and I made myself a new family, and I loved them. I know you probably don't want to hear that, but I did. It was a different love than what I had for y'all, but it was a true thing just the same. But I never forgot you. I never forgot any of you."

"I never forgot you, neither, Pap. I tried real hard, but I didn't."

"Thank you for that." I saw a bright light start to form out of the corner of my eye, and Pap turned to see it. "Looks like my train's 'bout to pull out of the station," he said.

"You stayed here just to tell me all that? What if I hadn't come?"

"You would, eventually." He smiled at me, got off the back of my truck, and walked into the light. It flashed brighter than the sun, then popped out, leaving me blinking and rubbing my eyes. I was alone in the cemetery, and I went back over to where the men had been running the backhoe, and I shed a tear over my pap's grave. Not for his death, but for the life we never shared.

I sat there for about an hour, just talking to Granny about Jenny, and Shelly, and the idiot Baptist preacher, and her soaps that I still watched every day so I could keep track of who's alive and dead for her. After a while, though, my knees started really giving me fits, and my spine started to knot up down in my lower back, so I got up and moseyed on back to the truck. I ran my fingers across the stones as I walked, liking the feeling of the different granites used. Some were buffed to a high polish, but plenty were either too old for that, or just never cared to pay for it.

I got to my truck and looked at myself in the mirror. I was born lucky—I have a complexion that lets me cry without turning into a red, blotchy mess. I fixed my makeup and put the truck in gear, pointing the old girl down the street toward the sheriff's office.

CHAPTER 10

I never made it to the sheriff's office. I stopped at Sharky's Pub, the one bar in town. Sheriff Dunleavy's car was parked out front between a Harley-Davidson and a Hyundai SUV. I pulled my truck into the gravel parking lot at the end of a string of cars and walked into the pub.

"Pub" is by far the most generous word ever applied to Sharky's. Most folks always called it "the beer joint," since it was the only licensed drinking establishment in town. Some of the more religious referred to it as "that place," but one thing nobody ever accused it of being was high class.

The squat cinderblock building had four windows across the front, and every one of them was plugged with air conditioning units. It was painted a sickly shade of beige, kinda somewhere between spoiled egg yolks and baby poop. The door was the only thing that ever looked fresh, on account of Sharky having to replace it about once a month when he put some drunk through it.

I stepped into the dim, smoky room, and Sharky looked up from the bar. "Hey there, Lila Grace," he called out, and conversation slammed to a halt. I was not a regular, but this was certainly not my first time in the bar. When there's only one place in town to get a cold beer that's not your own refrigerator, everybody who likes a nip now and then will pass through the doors.

"Hello, Stan," I called back. I think I was the only person in town that never called him Sharky. I just didn't like the name. I didn't think it fit. Stan was a trim man, slight of build and thin of mustache. He looked a lot more like a ferret than a shark, but he went away down to Florida to work construction one summer, and when he came back, he told us everybody down there called him Sharky. I doubt anybody ever called him Sharky a day in his life, but if it made him feel better, who was I to call him out on it? So after that, people called him Sharky.

The bar was about what you'd expect from a small-town joint in South Carolina. There were half a dozen stools with cracked pleather seats in front of a bar that had four beer taps on it. Sharky's served Budweiser, Bud Light, Miller Lite, and Coors on draft, and a couple more selections than that in the bottle. Corona was the sole nod to an import beer, but I knew Gene kept a six-pack or two of Red Stripe in the cooler for his personal use. There were two rows of bottles on the glass shelves behind the bar. The selections topped out at Jack Daniels and Jim Beam. Anything fancier than that or Grey Goose, and you were going to have to either drink it at home or drive to another town. Sharky also kept a few jars of Uncle Dargin's apple pie moonshine tucked away, and he'd bring that out on special occasions or for special customers.

Today must have been pretty special because there was a Ball jar sitting on the bar with the top off, and a shot glass in front of the sheriff and its brother in front of Stan. "Y'all having a little taste?" I asked, pulling out a stool to sit next to the sheriff.

"Just a little bit, Lila Grace. Y'all want some?" Stan asked. I nodded, and he pulled me up a shot glass from under the counter. He wiped it down with a rag, and I honestly wasn't convinced that took any germs or dirt off the glass. It looked like the rag started life a whole lot dirtier than the glass, but I wasn't too concerned. Uncle Dargin made his 'shine stout, and I figured it'd kill just about anything in the glass before it got my lips.

I took the offered drink from Stan and raised it to my lips. "May we be in Heaven half an hour before the devil knows we're dead," I said, and took a long sip of the moonshine. Apple pie ain't shooting 'shine, it's sipping liquor, and this batch was as smooth as any I'd ever had.

"That's good stuff, Stanley," I said, putting the glass down. "Tell Dargin I said so."

"I'll do it, Lila Grace," Stan said.

"Go see if Jerry needs a refill, Sharky," Sheriff Dunleavy said.

"Jerry passed slap out, Sheriff," Stan replied, not getting it. He had that problem in school, too. It caused him to repeat fifth grade a couple of times, and by the time he finally got through eighth grade, ol' Stan was through with schooling.

"Go check on him, Sharky." The growl in Dunleavy's voice left no question as to whether or not he was asking this time. Stan started, like he was surprised at something, then walked over to sit at a small table in the corner where Jerry Gardner was lying face down on the faux wood surface.

"What can I do for you, Ms. Carter?" the sheriff asked.

"I reckon I was going to ask you the same thing, Sheriff. You sitting in here all alone day drinking, I thought maybe you was in need of something."

"I am," he said. "I am in need of a drink. Then that drink might put me in need of another drink. I might even require a few more to follow that second one. I am almost certain by the time I get to five or six drinks I'll be just about right, but I'm liable to have two more after that just to make sure."

From the sounds of him, he'd already had more than one drink, but it wasn't my place to judge. I just sat there and sipped my apple pie. "You talked to Shelly's parents, I reckon."

"I did."

"That the first time you've had to notify parents their child has passed?"

"It was."

"I'm sorry."

"Me too."

The sheriff sat there for a minute, then poured himself another shot. I knocked back the last of my moonshine and held out my glass. Dunleavy looked at me sideways for a second, then topped it off.

"Don't go giving me the side-eye, Sheriff," I said. "I been drinking Dargin's home brew since I was a teenager fooling around in the back seat of Bobby Joe Latham's Chevrolet."

"I wouldn't have pegged you for a drinker, Ms. Carter," he said.

"Well, I ain't a professional at it, like you seem to be, but I can hold my own if I need to."

"What's that supposed to mean?" He turned to me like he wanted to say something else, but stopped.

"Which part?" I asked.

"That crack about me being a professional drinker. What did you mean by that?"

"I meant you've got two dead girls, no real leads, and instead of being out there trying to find out who killed them, you're in here drinking moonshine in the middle of the afternoon because some- body's mama or daddy hurt your feelings while you was doing your job. Well, I got news for you, Sheriff Dunleavy, you put on the badge, you strapped on that pistol, that means you get to take the bad days with the good ones. Most days, sheriffing in Lockhart ain't nothing but overnight drunk tank visits, spray paint from teenagers, and speeding tickets, but right now we need a real damn lawman, not some stereotype of a Sam Spade movie sitting in a bar like a moody little bitch."

I allowed as how calling the sheriff a bitch might have been exces- sive, but finding him hiding in a bar instead of out looking for a murderer riled me up a little.

"I don't appreciate your tone, Lila Grace," the sheriff said. He didn't look at me; that's how I knew he knew I was right.

"I don't give a good goddamn, Sheriff," I replied.

"Willis," he said.

"Excuse me?"

"My name. It's Willis. I reckon if I'm gonna call you Lila Grace, and we've got to the point where you're comfortable enough to read me out in a bar, we might as well be on a first name basis. So, you can call me Willis. Unless we're out in public doing something official. Then I'm still 'Sheriff.'" He stood up, tossed two twenties on the bar, and put his hat on.

"We're leaving, Sharky. I'm confiscating the rest of this jar of pie, though."

"Aw, come on, Sheriff," Gene whined. "That's my last jar!"

"I left you forty bucks for it, Shark. I know you don't pay Dargin but fifteen, so shut your cake hole." He walked out the front door.

I followed, nodding farewell to Sharky as I passed him. "Stan," I said.

"Bye, Lila Grace. Y'all come back now, ya hear?"

Like there was a single other option for a place to get a beer in this town.

CHAPTER 11

The police station was full when I walked in behind the sheriff. Deputy Jeff was standing behind the small wooden counter that served to separate the small area with four desks where he, Ava the Dispatcher, and Victor, the other deputy, sat. Half a dozen people were milling around the counter, every one of them trying to talk to Jeff.

Silence fell over the room when we entered; then it exploded into mayhem as everybody turned to Dunleavy all at once. I staggered back at the ruckus, almost walking right through Jenny. The girl was waiting in the truck for me when I walked out of Sharky's and rode to the station without a word. I reckon she was trying to process Shelly's death and trying to figure out why she was lingering while her friend moved on without her.

Sheriff Dunleavy held up his hands for quiet, and after a few seconds, the room settled down. "Now I know all y'all want to help, and I know everybody is anxious to share any information they have that might aid the investigation. But we ain't but a couple of people here, so we are going to have to follow some kind of order.

"I am going in to my office to consult with Ms. Carter here on some research she is doing for me on these investigations. I need all y'all to line up and give Jeff your information in an orderly fashion. Make sure he has your phone number written on the statement, and we will follow up with y'all as we move forward. Thank you all for coming out. I appreciate your assistance and patience in this trying time."

Sheriff Dunleavy put his hands down and bulled through the packed people. I followed along in his wake like a girl waterskiing behind a boat, and a minute later, we were sitting in his office with the door closed. The noise from the front was down to a dull roar, so I reckoned Jeff had it under control.

"Now what was so damned important that you had to pry me away from some very important drinking and haul me back here?" Sheriff Dunleavy asked as he took a seat behind his desk.

"I was over at the Miller house—"

"What?" he interrupted.

"I was asking Jenny's father some questions, and—"

"You were *what*?" He interrupted me again, and I turned my best Sunday School teacher scowl on him.

"I was asking Jenny's daddy if he had any idea who would want to hurt his daughter. Then her mama…" I stopped, because Sheriff Dunleavy's face was getting some kind of red, and I was a little scared he was going to blow a gasket. "Are you okay, Sheriff?"

"No, Ms. Carter, I am not okay. You mean to tell me you went to talk to the parents of the victim in what has recently been determined to be a murder investigation without my permission, without any official authority, and without any accompaniment?"

"Well, when you put it like that, I reckon it sounds pretty awful. But yes, that's what I did. He told me about a boy at school that may have had a grudge against Shelly for doing something nasty with his phone—"

"Ian Vernon," the sheriff said. "I had Victor interview him this morning."

"Oh, you knew about him? Good. Well, he also mentioned that we might want to talk to girls that—"

"—didn't make the cheerleading squad," he finished my sentence for me. "We have interviews scheduled with all of them for tomorrow at school. Of course, in light of today's events, we might have to post-pone those."

"If you know everything I'm going to say, why are you having me say it?" I asked. I was a little perturbed at his attitude.

"Because I'm trying to come up with a good reason not to charge you with interfering with a police investigation, obstruction of justice, and impersonating a police officer."

I stood up and put my hands on his desk. "What in the hell are you talking about, Sheriff? I was just trying to help you! All I did was talk to that poor man."

"That, and get his wife so riled up she called over here and told me that if anybody from my department set foot on her property again without somebody calling 911, that she'd sue us so hard we'd be writing tickets out of the back of a used Chevette." There was a little vein pulsing in his forehead, and his face was so red it was almost purple.

I sat back down, feeling like somebody had just let all the air out my sails. "Well...I'm sorry?"

Sheriff Dunleavy sat down and let out a huge breath. "You're sorry?"

"Yes, I'm sorry."

"That's all you've got?"

"What more would you like me to say? That it was a mistake? Well, obviously it was. That I'm sorry I upset the Millers? Well, I certainly am. That I won't do it again? I don't know that I'm going to say that, Sheriff."

"Oh, I reckon you are going to say that, Ms. Carter. You are going to say that, and you are going to mean that, and you are going to stay the hell away from this investigation. You are going to leave the police work to the police, and you are going to go home and prune your tomatoes, or whatever you do in the afternoons."

"You don't prune tomatoes, Sheriff," I said with a smile.

He didn't smile back. "I don't care. Obviously, what I'm saying is not getting through. You cannot be part of this investigation, Lila

Grace. You are not a police officer, and I let myself get caught up in your…unconventional sources of information and gave you an incorrect impression."

"What impression is that, Sheriff?"

"That you are part of this investigation. Which you are not. You are not working with the police. You are a private citizen, and you are going to do what private citizens do, which is to stay out of the way and let the police do our job. Do you understand me?"

I felt my lips purse, and I took a deep breath before I spoke. When I did, there was not a hint of a tremor in my voice. "I understand perfectly, Sheriff. I will stay out of your way from here on out. You have my word." I stood up, looked down at him, and asked, "Will there be anything else?"

"No, Ms. Carter," he said. "You can go. I do appreciate the help you have given us to this point. It has been very valuable."

"Thank you, Sheriff," I said, and turned to the door. I walked out through the office and pushed my way through the throng in the front of the counter. I stepped out into the bright sunshine and got into my truck, pulling out into the street and driving home without taking any notice of anything around me. Almost in a daze, I walked into my house, fixed myself a glass of sweet tea, and walked out onto my back porch. I sat down on the steps and looked out over the small vegetable garden I had coming up. Just half a dozen twenty-foot rows of tomatoes, beans, squash, and potatoes, with two pumpkin and three watermelon vines going wild at the end of the rows.

I sat there, sipping my tea and looking at my garden as I went over and over what the sheriff had said to me. I didn't like his tone, but I couldn't disagree with the facts as he presented them. I had overstepped. I never should have gone to the Miller house, and I certainly shouldn't have talked to Mr. Miller alone.

Who was I kidding? I was no detective, no Mayberry Miss Marple solving mysteries and bringing killers to justice. I was just a half-cracked old lady with a little bit of a talent for hearing dead people.

I stood up and made to go inside when I caught sight of Sheriff

Johnny standing on the other side of my screen door. Jenny was beside him, and both of them looked grim.

"What's the matter, y'all?" I asked, pulling the door open and stepping inside. I set the empty glass down by the sink and turned to look at my visitors from beyond.

"Please don't quit, Ms. Lila Grace," Jenny said. "I know the new sheriff was mean to you, and I heard what Mama said, but please." The child's voice took on a pleading tone. "There ain't nobody else that can see me, or hear me, and I know that if you quit looking, ain't nobody going to figure out who...who killed me, and now killed Shelly, too. I just know it!" The dishes rattled a little in the drying rack by the sink, testimony to the strength of the poor child's upset. She was actually able to interact with the material world, which took either a ghost of tremendous power or one that was very upset. Jenny certainly seemed to fall into the latter category.

"I don't know, darling," I said. "Could be Sheriff Dunleavy's right. I might be doing more harm than good, particularly where your parents are concerned. I had no right to go out there acting like some kind of TV detective and getting your daddy all upset."

Sheriff Johnny stepped forward and held up a hand, like he was telling me to stop. His lips started to move, and I shook my head. "Johnny, we both know you can't—"

He held up that hand again, and I closed my trap. He screwed up his face, like he was working really hard to think of something, then I heard it. His voice sounded like the wind whispering through a cemetery late at night, all kinds of rasp and hiss to it, but it was unmistakably his.

"You do good, Lila Grace," he whispered, and I could see his image dim with the exertion. "You can't stop. No one else will speak for usssss." The last word trailed off into a long hiss, and he turned and walked through my back storm door. I watched him walk off, fading into invisibility as he did.

"I thought you said he couldn't talk," Jenny said.

"I didn't think he could," I said. I heard my own voice sound hollow, like it was coming from a long way away, or through a tunnel or something.

I stood there, leaning with my back against the sink for several minutes before I finally gave myself a little mental shake and walked into the living room. I picked up a little yellow notepad from the table beside my recliner and waved for Jenny to sit on the couch over to my left. I angled the chair a little bit so I was facing her more than the TV, even though it was off. That way I could look at her and not have to turn my head the whole time.

"Sit down, sweetie, and let's get to work," I said. "We got a murderer to catch."

CHAPTER 12

An hour later, I had a list of suspects that didn't like Shelly, a list that didn't like Jenny, a list that might have a grudge against both of them, and a list of the kids at school that hated everybody and everything. I figured that list was nothing but a dead end, but if I was going to poke around in people's lives, I might as well be thorough.

I looked at the clock on the cable box, and it read half past five. Too late to find out anything at the school, so I decided to go talk to the one person who wasn't on either list, but was in both girls' lives. As much as I hated the idea, I had to go talk to Reverend Turner.

The manse at the First Baptist Church of Lockhart was a modest ranch on a small lot beside the church. I walked up the two steps on the porch and opened the screen door, then knocked twice. I heard Reverend Turner's wife call out from inside the house, and a few seconds later her, blond head appeared in the little rectangular pane of glass in the front door. She opened the door, a welcoming smile on her face.

"Well, hello, Lila Grace. How are you? What brings you by our place this time of day?"

"Hello, Mrs. Turner," I replied. "I do apologize for dropping by unannounced, and right here at suppertime, no less. I just need to have a word with Reverend Turner."

"Aaron? Well, let me just go get him for you. Do you want to come in? I was just putting supper on the stove, so it ain't gonna be ready to eat for a little while yet, but I could slice up a couple pieces of my lemon meringue pie if you'd like a little something." Marie Turner was one of those Southern women who thought every problem in the world could be solved with sweet tea and dessert. She was a Peach Queen over in Gaffney before she met the Reverend, who was a serious boy in school and grew up to be a serious man.

Marie was a lively child, and beautiful to boot, but years of small-town life and home visits beside the Reverend had turned her from a slight, active girl into a lively, smiling, round woman who bubbled over with enthusiasm about everything. She was, in short, one of the sweetest, happiest women I'd ever known. I had no idea how she maintained such a positive outlook on life being married to such an awful sourpuss as Aaron Turner.

The sourpuss himself came to the door when he heard my name, that perma-scowl carved into his face like granite. "What are you doing here, Lila Grace?" The little tufts of grey hair ringing his bald head almost vibrated in his obvious anger at me having violated his sacred private space. Never mind that his sacred private space was paid for by the congregation of his church, and he was paid a salary and some living expenses besides.

Aaron Turner was a rail-thin man, with the grumpy disposition most often found in the painfully thin. I've always imagined that going through life being made up of nothing but sharp edges and bony points could make one irritable, but as I've been a woman of some substance ever since my breasts came in when I was in middle school, I was spared that pain. He was in his middle forties, about a decade younger than me, but if you were to ask anyone, they would assume him to be older, as his hair was snow-white, what little bit there was left. His narrow hazel eyes squinted as he looked down on me, and I couldn't hold back a sigh.

"I need to speak with you, Reverend. Would you like to chat on the porch, or should I come inside?" I asked.

"Outside," he said. His voice was clipped and curt, but I knew that would be his answer. There was exactly one way that an official Servant of Satan like myself was going to get into his house, and that was in the dead of night creeping through a window. Since those days passed long ago, I stepped over to one of the rockers on his porch and took a seat.

"Should I get a couple glasses of iced tea?" Marie asked, her voice as sweet as a bird.

"No, we're fine," her husband snapped. "Go watch the food." Marie's face flushed, and she fled back inside the house.

"There's no need to be rude to her just because you don't like me," I said, mentally kicking myself for breaking my promise to myself with nearly the first thing I ever said to the man. The whole drive over, I'd been lecturing myself on ignoring his jibes and his little pokes at me and my Christianity and my gift. I'd been telling myself to stay on track, to not get distracted by his stupidity. So, of course, the first thing I do is get in his business about how he talks to his wife.

He whipped his head around to me, but then he took a deep breath and said, "You're right. I will make it a point to apologize to Marie when I go inside. But what can I do for you, Lila Grace?"

My mouth fell open. If there had been a fly buzzing by my head just then, it certainly would not have survived the trip. "Excuse me, Reverend?"

"No, excuse *me*, Lila Grace. I am working to become more inclusive in my thinking and my behavior, and despite the fact that I think you're either a charlatan or a fraud, and almost certainly bound for Hell once you die regardless of which, there is no cause for me to be as discourteous as I have been in the past."

I took a second to parse out exactly what he was saying, but after a minute, I was pretty sure I had it unwrapped. "So you're saying that you think I'm terrible and that I'm stealing people's money, but you're gonna stop being an asshole?"

"To put it crudely, yes."

"I'll take it," I said, extending a hand. The clearly uncomfortable minister shook it, and we leaned back to keep rocking. "I need your help, Reverend."

"I assume this concerns the deaths of poor Jenny and Shelly."

"It does."

"You are wondering if there was anything happening at church that may have led to their untimely passing."

"I am."

"You want me to tell you every intimate detail of their private lives, including anything that they may have confided to me in confidence."

"I ain't told that man nothing in confidence," Jenny said, standing right on the far side of the reverend's chair. "He's a jerk."

"I don't want you to violate your principles in any way, Reverend, but I do want to remind you that these girls are dead. Nothing you tell me can hurt them, but it might be the key to locking up the man that did them harm."

He sat there for a long minute, steepling his fingers on his belly like he was thinking, but I could tell all he was really doing was trying to make me sweat. Too bad for him I had lived too long to fall for that garbage. I sat there watching him patiently, not saying a word. If I've learned anything about men in my years on this planet, and you can decide for yourself if my lifelong spinsterhood says that I have learned nothing about men or that I have learned far too much about them, it is that they can't wait out a patient woman. Women go through hours of excruciating pain to bring life into this world. Men participate in a few minutes of the pleasurable part of childbirth. We women are wired for more patience.

"I will share the girls' confidences with you, but you must not divulge your source unless it is absolutely critical to apprehend the murderer. I cannot under any circumstances have my congregation thinking they can't trust me," Turner said, the piety dripping from every syllable.

I mentally counted to ten before I spoke, so I wouldn't say anything untoward and fracture this new and likely very fragile peace that the good reverend and I had wrought. "I would never let anybody know that any of my information came from you, Reverend. I will hold your words as close as the confessional." He looked a little askance at the mention of Catholicism, but I gave him my most grandmotherly smile, and he let it slide.

"Now, was there anybody that the girls mentioned to you as being particularly troublesome to them in any way?" I asked, leaning forward with my elbows on my knees.

"Jenny was much less…forthcoming than Shelly. Shelly was such a dear child," the preacher said, wiping a crocodile tear from the corner of his eye.

"What he meant was that Shelly dressed like a slut when she came to talk to him about stuff, and I didn't let him look down my shirt," Jenny said, leaning against the wall to the left of the reverend's chair.

I developed a sudden coughing fit to cover my laughter, and I grabbed my pocketbook from the floor next to me. I dug around in there, looking for a peppermint to help with my "coughing" and to hide my face from the preacher. I swear if I had looked at him right them, I probably would have laughed so hard I'd have spit a mint right in his eye.

"Are you okay, Lila Grace? Let me get Marie to fetch you a glass of tea." He got up and stuck his head in the kitchen door. His voice was muffled by my coughing and the door, but he came back with a glass of tea in a few seconds. Marie probably just grabbed one of the tea glasses set up for their supper, poor woman.

"Thank you," I said, taking a long drink. She made good tea. It obviously wasn't instant, that was good, and it had the right amount of sugar in it. Sweet, but not so much that it makes your teeth hurt. I smiled at Reverend Turner and motioned for him to proceed.

"Well, like I said, Shelly was more open than Jenny, but there were a few names that popped up whenever both girls talked about school."

"Who were they, Reverend?" I asked.

The reverend rattled off half a dozen names, all of them already on my legal pad. I dutifully wrote them down on a clean sheet of paper, just in case the source somehow became important later.

"Was there anybody at church, Reverend Turner?" I asked after he gave me all the people he could think of from school. I knew I had to go gentle with this because Turner was way more likely to be protective of his own "flock" than of some child from school he didn't know.

"There was an incident last summer on a youth group trip, but I don't believe it was anything serious." He looked uncomfortable, like he didn't really want to talk about it, which made me think it certainly fell into the category of "things Lila Grace wants to know." I was also intrigued because it happened a year ago, was a big enough deal that the preacher remembered it, and Jenny hadn't mentioned it to me before.

"Why don't you just tell me about it, Reverend? If it turns out to be nothing, then at least we know," I said. I took a huge chance and leaned forward, patting him on the knee. He didn't burst into flame, something I'm sure came as a huge surprise to him. He also didn't leap to his feet shouting "Sinner!" which surprised me no small amount.

He looked around, as if to make sure we were alone. Like somebody was going to hide in my azaleas to snoop on an old lady talking to a preacher. "I heard from one of the chaperones that he caught the girls in one of the boys' rooms after they were all supposed to be in bed for the night, and there was beer involved. It was even said that... one of the girls may have been topless!" His eyes got big, and I bit down on the inside of my cheek real hard to keep from laughing in his face.

Imagine that, a bunch of teenagers go to the beach and they find some way to get beer. Horror of horrors, one or more of them even ends up naked! I guess if there was sex involved and somebody got jealous, that could cause a problem. Or if somebody got pregnant... I sighed and turned my attention back to Turner, who sat on the edge of his seat with the prurient anticipation of someone who got to do their favorite thing in the world—tattle.

"Thank you, Reverend. That could be very important. Do you have a list of the children on the trip?"

CHAPTER 13

I left the manse thirty minutes later with about half a dozen new names on my list and a plan of action in my head. I drove back across town to my church and pulled into a parking space this time, instead of letting the vehicle sit there all catty-wumpus like I was some kind of drunk driver.

"What are we doing here?" Jenny asked, passing through the door as I got out and closed mine.

"I've got a couple people I need to talk to, and this is the best place to do it," I said, walking across the grass, being careful to keep my steps to the narrow path between the foot markers and the row of headstones behind. I knew full well the people in the graves didn't mind me walking on them, I'd been told as much many times, but Mama always told me it was disrespectful to step on a grave, so I tried my best not to.

Uncle Luther was sitting on his headstone, like he was about every night. I didn't have any idea where he went during the day, and really had no idea why he was lingering. Luther couldn't speak, and no time in all my trips through the cemetery had he ever tried to flag me down or communicate with me at all. He just sat on that headstone every night, watching the street like he was waiting for somebody. It couldn't be Aunt Lula—she passed ten years ago and didn't linger a minute, just went straight on into the light the second her soul stood up from her body. Luther just sat there, night after night, not bothering nothing, so I didn't see as how it was any of my business.

I made a beeline for Helen Good's plot. Helen was part of the town switchboard when she was living, and that didn't change a bit when she died. The switchboard was what the locals called a network of old women who all went to church together, usually over at the Methodist church, and talked on the phone every morning. Whenever an ambulance or fire truck went down the road, you could be sure that Miss Helen, Miss Faye Russell, or Miss Frances Wyatt knew the whys and the wherefore of what was going on within five minutes of it happening.

Since she died, Miss Helen had become an even more important source of news and gossip around town. She was a rare ghost, one that wasn't tied to one place, could talk, and didn't seem to have any desire to move on. I asked her about it once, but all she would say was that Lockhart was her home, and it was her duty to keep an eye on things. I reckon it might have had more to do with her widower Mr. George and the fact that he had taken to stepping out with Julia McKnight about three months after Miss Helen was in the ground. After that happened, her little round ghostly form could often be seen flitting back and forth between her home and the McKnight place, trailing one of her long, flowered dresses through the air like a Laura Ashley printed Casper.

Miss Helen was at home, so to speak, when I walked up. She was at her stone, standing with her arms folded watching the goings on around the cemetery. At any given time, there were a dozen or more regulars hanging around a church cemetery in any small town, and First Presbyterian was no different. Miss Helen was the unofficial mayor of the First Presbyterian dead, and she smiled as she saw me coming.

"Oh good Lord, child, come here and let me get a look at you!" She squealed a little when I approached. She once confided to me that she got a little bored with the conversations she had in the cemetery and looked forward to my visits since I was alive and could actually talk *with* her, instead of just talking at her, like her daughter and granddaughter had to do. The dead are typically very much locked in to the world and opinions they held when they died, so I could see how talking to ghosts all the time could get boring. I often wished that the ghosts I talked to could be a little more boring and little less murdered.

"Hey Miss Helen, how you doing today?" I said. Had she been alive, she would have hugged my neck. As it was, we just gave each other awkward little waves on account of her insubstantiality.

"Fine, I'm fine, darling. Hope you are. And who is this little darlin'?" she asked, looking at Jenny.

"I'm Jenny Miller, ma'am. Pleased to meet you." Jenny stuck out her hand.

"Oh sweetie, I'm sorry, but—" Helen's mouth fell open as Jenny was able to touch her and shake her hand. "Oh my goodness, honey, I am *so* sorry! You know sometimes it is so hard to tell who is who, especially with y'all that ain't been gone very long."

Helen turned back to me. "What in the world is going on, Lila Grace? Why did you bring this dead child to my plot? Do you need some help, honey?"

I wasn't sure whether she was talking to me or Jenny, but maybe it was both, so I just said, "Yes, Miss Helen. I do need some help. Jenny here was murdered last week, and I was hoping maybe you could help us figure out who did it."

"Oh, sweetie, I am so sorry!" Helen reached out and wrapped Jenny in a big-armed, muumuu-wearing hug that probably would have suffocated the child, or at least popped a rib, if she'd still been drawing breath. As it was, she was fine.

"Thank you, ma'am. I appreciate that," Jenny said.

"Miss Helen, were you anywhere near the Miller place last Friday?" I asked.

"I don't think so. Which one is the Miller house?" she asked.

"It's over on Maple Lane, the brick house with the blue shutters," Jenny said.

"Oh yes, I know that place. What an unfortunate decision about them shutters. I really think they could have done better than that baby blue; it just clashes with the brick in all kinds of ways. I'm sorry, honey, I know that's your home and all, but it just ain't attractive."

"No, ma'am, don't be sorry. You're right. Mama told Daddy when he bought that paint they were going to be butt-ugly, and she was right," Jenny agreed.

"Okay, now I know the place. No, I wasn't anywhere close. I was over watching the ball game. Is that when you died, sweetie?" Helen asked, turning her head to Jenny.

"Yes, ma'am," Jenny answered. She turned to me, confusion all over her face. "How is it she can see and talk to me?"

"Well, honey. It's just like you could talk to Sheriff Johnny. Y'all all exist in the same plane. Of course she can see you," I explained.

"Lila Grace is too sweet to say that there ain't been nothing happening in Lockhart for forty years that me and my girls ain't seen," Helen said with a laugh. Two other ethereal women appeared to stand next to Helen, all three of them with broad smiles on their faces.

"She's too polite to say that not even the grave can shut your big old mouth, Helen," a slight, woman with a boyish haircut and a broad smile said, her grin denying her waspish words.

"Oh, be nice, Faye," the other woman said, a twinkle in her eye. She was a big woman, not round, like Miss Helen, but tall and imposing. There was a presence to her that hadn't diminished, even in death.

"Ladies," I said with a nod and a smile. "How y'all doing this evening?"

"Fine, fine," Faye Russell said with a nod, her bright blue eyes set deep in a wrinkled face. She wore much the same clothes she had on most days in life, a white striped blouse and a pair of blue jeans.

"We're all just excited to have some company with something to talk about other than how they died," Miss Frances said. She wore a bright red and white floral blouse with dark slacks and comfortable shoes, the kind of outfit I'd expect to see on a woman attending a church meeting, which Miss Frances did quite a bit of before she passed.

"Speaking of that, I need to talk to y'all about how this poor child died," I said to peals of laughter from the trio.

"Of course you do, sweetheart," Miss Helen said. "You wouldn't be here if you didn't need the assistance of the greatest investigators in Union County."

"Or the nosiest bitches in the Carolinas, if you want to be more accurate," Miss Faye said with a wry twist to her lips.

"Ignore those two, precious," Miss Frances said to Jenny. "What do you need to know? If we don't know it, we can probably find it out for you."

She wasn't kidding, either. Being dead had done nothing to quell these women's curiosity, and since a fair portion of their gossip network was also dead, they had a finger on the pulse of the town, as ironic as that sounds.

"We've got a bunch of people, and I need to know where they were Friday night," I said, showing the women our list of people who might hold grudges against the girls. "Anybody we can eliminate from suspicion in Jenny's murder is almost certainly innocent of Shelly's as well, and that will be better, since we don't have a good timeline on when Shelly died yet."

"Oh, that poor child, drowned in her car like that," Miss Faye said.

"We don't know that yet, Faye," Miss Helen said. "They ain't done with the autopsy yet. She might have been dead before she ever rolled into the lake."

"She's right," I agreed. "I hadn't considered that before, but the lake might have just been a place to dump the body and not where Shelly was killed."

"Well, that would be good," Miss France said.

"Why's that?" Jenny asked.

"With as many hollers and old gullies and patches of woods as we've got around here, if they pushed her car into the lake to hide the body, then the killer is either stupid or ain't from around here. Either one is good for us," the woman said.

"She ain't wrong," Miss Helen agreed. "Okay, Lila Grace, hold up that list. We'll memorize it and put the Dead Old Ladies' Detective Agency on the case!"

They took another look at the paper, then each of them nodded at me. The women went off in three different directions to talk to the dead in their relative cemeteries. I turned to Jenny and said, "Well, if there's anything known about your murder by any ghost in this part of the county, we'll know it in a few hours."

"What's next for us?" Jenny asked.

"Well, sweetie, I reckon next for me is going to be a bite of supper. I ain't had nothing to eat in a considerable time, and my belly's going to start gnawing on my backbone if I don't correct that oversight in the immediate future." I walked to the truck and got in. "Besides, I think Sheriff Dunleavy owes me an apology, and maybe a steak dinner."

CHAPTER 14

Sheriff Dunleavy's car was one of about half a dozen parked in front of Sharky's when I pulled up. I parked at the end of a row to make sure I wouldn't have any trouble getting out, since I didn't plan on staying long. Jenny cocked her head at me when I turned off the truck and opened the door.

"I thought you said you were hungry."

"I am hungry," I replied.

"Well, Sharky's don't serve food," the girl said.

"How would you know? You ain't never going to get old enough to go into a beer joint."

"You act like anybody's checked an ID in Sharky's in, like, ever. All you need to get beer in there is have a single hair on your chin or on your—"

"Young lady!"

"I was gonna say legs, but that works, too." She gave me a saucy grin. "Now why are you really going in there?"

"Like I said, I think the good sheriff owes me an apology and a steak dinner for being rude to me earlier, and I plan to collect both of those things." I closed the truck door with a hollow metal *thunk* and walked across the gravel parking lot to Sharky's door. I looked down at what I was wearing and grimaced a little. I was in my normal weekday attire of a patterned shirt and blue jeans, with a pair of flat white tennis shoes. I didn't look *bad*, but it wasn't any real surprise from my wardrobe that I hadn't had very many dates this century. Well, I wasn't there to use my feminine wiles on the sheriff, even if he was a handsome, strapping man with a conspicuous lack of a wedding ring.

Every head in the dim room turned to me when I pushed open the door. Sharky did a double-take, then jerked his head over to the right to where the sheriff sat in a booth with his back to the wall. It wasn't like I couldn't see him. Sharky's place wasn't very big, and there weren't but about eight booths and four tables in the place. Somehow, I would have been able to figure out where Dunleavy was sitting among the ten people that were scattered through the room.

Even so, I walked in that direction without bothering to pretend I was here to see anybody else. Hell, the only person besides Stan that I knew well enough to speak to in a beer joint was Edith Hardcastle, and she and I weren't on the best speaking terms after she made disparaging remarks about my cherry pie three years ago at the Homecoming lunch after church. That biddy had the audacity to say I used a store-bought crust! I learned how to make that crust from my Gran in 1975 and have been rolling it by hand ever since I was tall enough to see over the counter. So I gave Edith a frosty nod as I walked over to see the sheriff.

"Bring me a bourbon, Stan," I said as I walked past the bar. "And not any of that Ancient Age shit, either. If you're out of Knob Creek, just bring me Turkey."

I slid into the booth across from Dunleavy and gave him a smile. "Good evening, Sheriff. How are you doing?"

He just sat there, watching me with a baleful eye. "What do you want, Lila Grace?"

"Why do I need to want anything, Sheriff? Can't I just come by and have a drink with a friend? Thank you, Stan. What do I owe you?" I said, taking my glass.

"Lila Grace, you know I ain't gonna take your money," Sharky said.

"I know, Stan, but it's polite to offer, and I hold out hope that one day you'll forget and let me start buying my drinks again."

"Not gonna happen, ma'am. But thank you." Stan turned and walked back to the bar, leaving me alone with the sheriff again.

"What did you do to him?"

"I think you mean 'for,'" I corrected.

"Excuse me?"

"I think you mean, what did I do *for* him, Sheriff. His mama passed, and she couldn't move on because she didn't leave a will, and there was some dispute between Stan and his brother Robert about what to do with her property. I called the three of them together and relayed his mama's wishes to them, and they got over their differences and did what she told them to do. Stan credits me with saving his relationship with his brother, which was rapidly deteriorating on account of the money involved."

"So you drink for free?"

"That was my fee, Sheriff," I explained. "I don't often charge people for what I do. I barter a great deal, and sometimes people do give me money, but usually I do what I do for one of two reasons. Either I have an overwhelming sense of justice and cannot let a wrong stand if I have the opportunity to make it right..."

"Or?"

"Or I have got some damn fool ghost hanging around at all hours irritating the ever-loving pee out of me to make things right with their loved ones."

"Which one is this?" he asked, sipping on his drink. It looked like a Jack and ginger from what I could see, and to smell his breath, it wasn't the first sample he'd taken of Lynchburg's finest since he'd got off work.

"Excuse me?" I asked.

"Which is this, Lila Grace? Are you poking around in Jenny Miller's death because you can't stand to see justice ignored, or because that poor dead girl won't leave you alone?"

"I'm going to ignore that question, Sheriff, and move on to the reason I am here. I—"

"Don't," he said. He didn't move, just sat there, his elbows on the table and his eyes trained on the glass in front of him.

I took a closer look at the sheriff. He had aged since this morning. A fine brown-and-gray stubble poked out across his face. His shirt wasn't creased, and there was a little gravy spot on his tie. All in all, it looked like he slept in his clothes, or didn't sleep at all. I figured one of those was true. Sheriff Johnny spent more than one night laying stretched out in one of the two cells in back, trying to catch a few winks in the middle of a tough case. Looked like Sheriff Dunleavy was doing the same thing.

I thought for a moment before I spoke. "Don't what, Sheriff? Don't ignore the question that you only asked because you want me to feel as miserable as you do right now? Don't come back here and try to help you because I have contributions to your case that nobody else has? Or just don't act like I give a damn what happens to my town? What do you not want me to do, Sheriff? So I can be sure of exactly what I am telling you to kiss my ass over."

His head snapped up and his brow furrowed, making a razor-sharp vertical line in the center of his brow. "Woman, I swear to—"

His mouth snapped shut and his eyes went wide as my palm cracked across his face like a rifle shot. "If I wanted to be spoken to like that, I could have married one of these rednecks around here. If you have something to say to me, you can call me Lila Grace, or you can call me Ms. Carter. But if you call me 'woman' like it's an insult again, you can be damn sure there'll be a matching handprint on the other side of your face."

Dunleavy leaned forward, one elbow on the table, his eyes blazing. He stuck one finger out at me and started wagging it as he talked. "I should have you arrested for—"

"You want to keep that finger, you best put it away," I said, my voice cold.

He stared at me long enough for it to be downright uncomfortable until he either decided we were both out of line, I was right, or that he wouldn't likely be walking out of that bar full of hillbillies if he laid hands on the woman that taught most of them in Vacation Bible

School when they were young'uns. He put his finger down and leaned back against the cracked and split red Naugahyde of the booth.

"Lila Grace, I am starting to wonder if I was brought to this town as penance for something I did in a past life because I cannot for the life of me think of anything I did to deserve you in my life."

"Sheriff, I assure you, there is nothing that you could do to deserve me." I smiled as I said it, and he just shook his head.

A rueful chuckle escaped his lips, and he picked up the glass of brown liquid on the table in front of him and knocked it back. He waved at Sharky for another, then gaped at me when I shook my head. "What's wrong, Lila Grace, you don't approve of me getting drunk? I assure you I do not intend to drive home intoxicated."

"Sheriff, as pleased as I am to hear that you do not intend to wrap your patrol car around a white oak tree between here and your house tonight, and as little as I would generally object to you crawling inside a bourbon bottle on your personal time, I am afraid that you have other obligations this evening. Obligations that require you to maintain at least a modicum of sobriety."

He raised an eyebrow at me, then held up a twenty to Stan. The bartender nodded and came over with the check. "That'll be fifteen, Sheriff."

"Keep the change, Sharky," Dunleavy said. Gene smiled and nodded, then took away our glasses and headed back to the bar.

"What, pray tell, are these obligations, Ms. Carter?"

"You are taking me to dinner," I said. The butterflies in my stomach were migrating north, south, and sideways all at the same time, despite my internal protestations that this was not a date, that I had no interest in this man outside the professional, and that all I wanted out of him was a free meal and an apology.

"I am?" Dunleavy asked with a slight smile. "Why exactly am I going to do that? And did you have a place in mind, or do I at least get some input?"

"You are taking me to dinner to apologize for your atrocious behavior this afternoon. You are paying for dinner *and* dessert to apologize for your behavior this evening, and no, you do not have any choice in where we go to eat. There are only five restaurants in this part of the county, as I'm sure you know, and only one of them can prepare a steak with any semblance of skill. So you are taking me to The Garden Cafe."

"I've heard the spaghetti at the Pizza Empire is real good," he countered.

"You are not apologizing to me at any place with checkered vinyl tablecloths. I will settle for nothing less than white linen. Or at least someplace with cloth napkins. Our choices are limited, after all."

"Well, if that is what I must do, then that is what I must do," he said, sliding out of the booth and standing up. He wobbled a little, not too bad, but just a little. "Why don't you drive?" he said, putting a hand on the back of the booth seat. "I can pick up my car later."

"Good choice, Sheriff. I would hate to have to report you to the authorities." I stood up and preceded him toward the door. Every eye in the place was on us as we walked out, the crazy ghost lady and the new sheriff. This would be all over the grapevine, living and dead varieties, within the hour.

"Y'all come back soon," Stan called as I opened the door. I threw a hand up over my shoulder in farewell and stepped out into the evening air.

CHAPTER 15

Tommy Braxton waved at us from the bar when we walked into The Garden Cafe. I was a bit underdressed for the clientele Tommy wanted to attract but about right for the clientele he actually had, so I didn't mind sitting down in the closest thing that part of Union County had to a fancy steakhouse. Sheriff Dunleavy even pulled my chair out for me like a real gentleman and everything.

Leslie, Tommy's youngest daughter, came over as soon as we were settled and handed us menus. There were about three other tables occupied, two of them with elderly couples having dinner so they could drive home before it got too late, and one a family with a young child sitting in a booster seat and trying in vain to have a decent dinner out with a toddler. I figured it was their first child and they just didn't know any better. In a couple years, they'd be fine, but right now everything the poor little boy did was either a crisis or the greatest thing in the world.

I have always loved children; it's why I spent so many years teaching Sunday School and Vacation Bible School. When I was a child myself, I wanted to grow up, get married, and have a house just bursting at the seams with young'uns.

But as I grew older, I realized that my particular gifts make it hard to keep a relationship, thanks to odd hours that ghosts decide to visit me and the general creepiness that most people see in somebody who actually converses with dead people, instead of just talking at them like most folks do. Add to that the unfortunate tendency of lingering ghosts to be nosy as hell, and I was not what most people would consider a "catch." So, children weren't really in the cards for me. But I have been blessed with hundreds of boys and girls who love their "Miss Lila Grace," and most of the time that's been enough for me.

"Never wanted any or never had the chance?" Willis asked.

My head whipped back around to look at him, and he just gave me a wistful smile. "Same here," he said. "I always wanted them, but my ex-wife didn't, and now it just seems a little late in the game."

"I reckon that is one of the hazards of having dinner with a detective, ain't it?" I asked. "He's liable to know more than you want to let on."

"Could be, except I'm not a detective anymore. I reckon I'm as close as what we've got for this mess, but if I'd wanted to keep dealing with murderers, I would have stayed in Milwaukee."

"Is that where you're from, Sheriff?"

"Willis," he corrected.

"I'm sorry. Is that where you're from, *Willis?*"

He gave me one of those little half-smiles again, the kind he had started doing when he knew I was being a smart-aleck but didn't want to call me out on it. I kinda liked it. "That's not where I'm from, originally, but I lived and worked there for thirty years, so I reckon it's kinda where I'm from now."

"Where are you from, originally?" I asked.

"Carrboro," he said. "Just outside Chapel Hill."

"I know it," I said. "I knew a girl from there when I was in school. We went to Winthrop together."

"I didn't know you went to college," he said.

"I did. I graduated with a bachelor's degree in English literature and proceeded to do nothing with it for most of my adult life," I said.

"Never wrote the Great American Novel," he asked, that teasing smile back for a second.

"No, I never wanted to be a writer. I thought I would teach, but that didn't work out for me." That brought back some unpleasant memories, and I guess they showed on my face, because Dunleavy wasted no time in poking that sore spot.

"What happened?" he asked. I looked up at him, and he shrugged. "If you don't want to talk about it, that's fine. I just thought it might be better dinner conversation than dead girls in cars in lakes."

Of course, the second he says the words "dead girls," Tommy's girl walks up with her little notepad out to take our food orders. The poor child looked so scandalized I couldn't decide whether to laugh or cry, so I decided to fake a coughing fit and run to the bathroom, leaving Willis on his own to dig his way out of that one. It served him right, sticking his nose into everybody's business. I washed my hands, splashed a little cold water on my face, and freshened up my lipstick before I walked back to the table, mostly composed.

"I hope you like escargot," Willis said as I sat back down. "Because I ordered you an anchovy appetizer with an escargot main course. It's the least I could do to thank you for leaving me in that mess."

"I love snails," I said, hoping desperately that he was teasing, but completely unwilling to ask him if he was.

"Just like I love explaining to high school girls that I am not a serial killer while their father has his hand on a sawed-off shotgun under the bar," he said.

"I believe you were telling me about growing up in Carrboro," I said, changing the subject.

"I wasn't, but I will. I grew up there and went to Chapel Hill. I studied political science and was looking at law school when I decided to become a cop instead."

"What brought on that change?" I asked.

"A kid I grew up with got shot in the head trying to buy coke from the wrong guy in the wrong part of town. The Durham police didn't have a lot of time to look into the case of another dead black kid that summer, so I decided I'd become a cop to try and keep that from happening to anybody else."

"That's admirable," I said. He looked up at me to see if I was picking at him again, but his shoulders relaxed when he saw I was sincere. I was, too. A life of putting yourself in harm's way for the benefit of others is nothing to sneer at.

"Well, when I applied, I couldn't get a job at any of the departments near home, and my dad had a sister who lived in Milwaukee. So, I went to live with Aunt Gina for a while, got a job as a beat cop in the city, and worked my way up. Put in my thirty, got my city pension, and decided to come back home where I wouldn't ever have to shovel snow again."

"And where there's a lot less chance of somebody shooting at you," I added.

"That was a part of the thinking, yes. I'm not as fast as I used to be, so I wanted to go somewhere that the pace was a little slower, and a little safer. A man gets past fifty, he starts to think he probably wants to see sixty or seventy. A big city police department is no easy place to get old."

"A woman does the same thing, Sheriff," I said.

"You've heard," he said.

"What does that mean?" I asked.

"Lila Grace, you play the old woman card pretty well, but if you're a day over forty-five, I'll eat my hat."

I blushed a little. It had been a *long* time since a man commented positively on the way I looked, especially given my typical style of dress, and I had to admit, it felt good. I tried not to show it, though, as I grinned across the table at Willis. "Do you want some Texas Pete, or A-1 sauce, Sheriff? Because I'm fifty-seven years old and proud of every one of them."

"Well, I reckon there is something to be said for clean living after all because you sure don't look it," he said.

"Thank you, Willis. You haven't done too badly yourself, for an old coot." We both grinned a little bit. That break in the conversation turned out to be well-timed, as that's when our steaks came out. Mine was thankfully lacking in snails, but there was a nice dash of sautéed mushrooms scattered across my ribeye.

We dug in, and after I had a few bites of delicious steak in me, I asked, "So how did you end up all the way down here? Were you reading obituaries nationwide looking for dead sheriffs and police chiefs?"

He looked a little abashed, but chuckled as he said, "Well, almost. I set up a Google search for municipal job listings for a sheriff or chief of police position in a town of less than fifty thousand. This one popped up, and the county council was pretty happy to have somebody with my experience apply. Nothing against Sheriff Johnny, but the impression I got was that he wasn't the most up-to-date in his techniques."

I almost spit sweet tea across the table at him laughing. "You could say that. Johnny kept a baseball bat autographed by Buford T. Pusser hanging on the wall of his office. That was his hero, and his favorite movie was *Chiefs*. A fine piece of literature, I will agree, but not exactly what I'd call the forefront of police methodology."

"What happened to him?" Willis asked. "I get that it wasn't anything in the line of duty, but nobody seems willing to discuss it. Was he out with the wrong woman, or something?"

I laughed again. If he kept this up, the poor man was going to think I thought he was a moron. "No, nothing like that. I reckon it would be a little embarrassing because he was caught with his pants down, after a fashion. Johnny was a fisherman, and he liked his liquor, like most fishermen do. Hell, most *people* around here like a drink or two. Well, Johnny was out in his little bass boat just tooling along Broad River, and he had him a jar, like he would most Sunday mornings. Johnny wasn't much of a church-goer, you know. He said he felt like if God needed him, he'd know where to find him. Well, I reckon God needed him because that Sunday morning, he found him, and he took him, right there in his boat."

"What's embarrassing about that? The fact that he was drinking? I can't imagine anybody would care about that," he said.

"Well," I hesitated before going on, then I figured he was going to hear it eventually, might as well be over a good meal. "It wasn't so much the drinking, or the fishing, as it was the fact of exactly how he went that might be considered less than dignified."

Willis made one of those "go on" motions with his hand and took a sip of tea with his other. I waited for him to swallow before I went on, not relishing the idea of getting a face-full of the sweet beverage.

"He fell out of the boat taking a leak, hit his head on a rock, and drowned," I said it all in a rush, so as to get it out all at once, like ripping off a bandage.

Willis did what just about everybody that hears the story of poor Sheriff Johnny's demise does. He stared at me for a second, then his shoulders shook, kinda like a convulsion, then he couldn't hold it back anymore, and the laughter just blew right out of him like a cannonball. He laughed for about a solid minute before he wiped his eyes with his napkin and got himself under control.

"That has got to be the craziest death story for a cop I have ever heard, and like I said, I been at this for better than thirty years. I've heard more than one story about somebody getting caught with his pants down, but there's usually a jealous husband, or wife, involved in those. This has got to be the first time I've ever heard of death by pissing. Damn, no wonder the poor man can't move on. He's got a lot to atone for before he feels like his legacy is secure again."

I gave a little chuckle of my own. "Oh, that ain't why Johnny's sticking around."

"So why is he still here? Waiting on somebody to catch the catfish that ate his nuts?"

"Don't be crude," I said. He held up both hands in apology, and I gave him a little grin to let him know that if it was crude, it was at least a little funny, too. "No, he's just here until he decides if you're a good enough replacement. If not, he'll be here 'til somebody better comes along."

Willis leaned back in his chair and folded his arms across his chest. "Huh," he said, a thoughtful look crossing his face. "He really loved this town, didn't he?"

"The Thomases have been in Union County since they came over from England. His people have been here for hundreds of years. There's a whole row of the cemetery with nothing but his kin. So yeah, he loved this place and its people. Still does, as a matter of fact."

He leaned forward, fixing me with those deep brown eyes. "You do too, don't you?"

I thought for a second before I answered. "I do. It don't matter if not all of them love me. It don't matter if some of them think the things I can do make me a bad person or mean I'm in league with some dark power. For every one of them, there's somebody like Stan over at Sharky's. Somebody I can help when nobody else can."

"Somebody like Jenny Miller," Willis said, his voice soft.

"Somebody just like Jenny Miller," I agreed.

"You know we'll find him, right, Lila Grace?"

"The killer?" I asked. "Yeah, I know. We'll find him, and we'll make sure he pays for what he did to those poor girls."

"Yes, we will. But right now, I think we have something more important to focus our attention on." He sat up a little straighter and motioned Tommy's little girl over to the table. He smiled at the child when she arrived and gave me a wink.

"And just what could that be, Sheriff?" I was starting to enjoy this side of Sheriff Willis Dunleavy. He was a sharp man, one that could be deep in conversation one second and light-hearted and teasing the next. The man had layers. I liked that.

"Dessert, Lila Grace. We need to decide if we want to try the apple cobbler or the pecan pie."

"Well, I do have you at an unfair advantage here, Sheriff," I replied, smiling at the waitress. "Because I happen to know that this girl's Granny Hope made a fresh peach cobbler just this afternoon because I saw her this morning on the way to Farmer Black's peach shed, and there ain't nothing better this side of the county than Theresa Hope's peach cobbler. So why don't you get us a couple plates of that, darling, and you won't even have to bother telling us about it?"

The girl grinned and turned around with a little flounce. "Yes ma'am, and I'll be sure to tell Granny what you said about her cobbler. She'll really appreciate it."

I leaned forward when the girl was out of earshot. "That child's grandmother thinks I had sexual congress with the devil himself to learn how to talk to dead people. Poor girl is going to be praying until daylight if she mentions my name in her presence. The old biddy can make a cobbler like nobody's business, though."

CHAPTER 16

We walked out of the restaurant and down the steps, our feet crunching in the gravel. "Well, I reckon this is goodnight, Lila Grace," Willis said, turning to me. He had that awkward look of a man that ain't sure if he's supposed to hug me, shake my hand, or try to kiss me.

I just wore my normal expression. Sheriff Johnny used to say I looked like I knew something he didn't. I replied that I usually did. "Why should this be goodnight, Sheriff?" I asked with a smile. I leaned back against the fender of my old truck and gave him a direct look.

He spluttered a little bit before he managed to spit out "W-well, I reckon it don't have to be, I mean, um…"

"You mean you still need a ride back to your car?" I said with one eyebrow up.

"Huh?" He looked for all the world like a bulldog chewing on a wasp, like there was something hurting his head, but he wasn't real sure what it was.

"We left your car at Sharky's, Willis. Unless you feel like walking three miles across town to go get it, I reckon you ain't getting rid of me that easy." I pushed off from the truck, reached out and closed his mouth with two fingers under his chin, and walked around to get into the driver's seat.

He slid in on the passenger side of the big bench seat and put on his seatbelt. "Don't you ever lock your truck?"

"Why in the world would I? This truck is better than thirty years old, has almost four hundred thousand miles on it, a rusted-out rear fender, and a bed held together pretty much with Bondo and paint. I don't keep anything in it worth stealing, except the shotgun behind the seat, and if there's anybody in the county that don't already have something better than a double-barrel four-ten, well, I reckon they're welcome to it." I pulled the truck out onto the highway in the wake of a log truck hauling a late load of pine. I love the smell of fresh-cut pine logs, but I did hang back far enough not to get sap on my windshield.

"You keep a shotgun behind the seat of your truck? You know that's against the law, right?"

"It ain't loaded, Willis. The shells are in the glove box, and it's locked. Usually. Sometimes. Well, at least the shells are in the glove box," I said. "Besides, what are you going to do, arrest an old woman for concealing a three-foot long shotgun? Judge Comer would laugh your ass right out of his courtroom."

He chuckled and rolled his window down, letting the warm air and the scent of honeysuckle filter into the truck's cab. "You ain't wrong, there. I swear that man thinks I ain't nothing more than a Yankee carpetbagger. He all but said so the first time I went to the courthouse to introduce myself."

"Well, maybe if that wasn't the first time I'd heard you say 'ain't' in the time I've known you, people wouldn't think you such an interloper."

"Now come on, that's not fair," he protested. "You use just as many big words as I do, if not more."

"That's true, but I have the benefit of living my entire life below the Mason-Dixon Line. You are at the distinct disadvantage of having spent three decades in Wisconsin, a place as foreign to most residents of the South Carolina Upstate as Kathmandu. Besides, I say all those big words with an accent. Gives it style."

We both laughed, and I pulled into the parking lot of Sharky's. There were a lot more cars in the lot now, but plenty of space around Willis's cruiser. Seemed like nobody wanted to risk having one too many and clipping the police car on the way out of the lot.

"You want to come in, have a nightcap?" he asked, opening the passenger door and slipping off his seatbelt.

"No, I think I better get home. All them cats get ornery if I stay out too late."

His face got a panicked look. "You have cats?"

I busted out laughing. "Lord, no! But I thought it would be funny to pretend to be the stereotypical crazy cat lady for a minute. No, I don't have any pets. They don't like all my unannounced visitors. Cats don't like ghosts, and I don't like cat pee on my hardwoods. Dogs are too stupid to care about random dead people showing up, and that means they're too dumb for me to tolerate. So, no pets for me. But I'm still gonna pass on that drink. Two glasses of wine with dinner has me feeling just right. I think I'm going to go home, take a bubble bath with a trashy romance novel, and go to sleep with the ceiling fan on."

"Sounds good," he said. He walked around the side of the truck and leaned in my open window. "I had a nice time tonight, Lila Grace. Does this clear my debt, or do I need to keep apologizing?"

I leaned forward a little. "I reckon I've almost forgiven you."

He moved closer. "Well, that means I've still got some work to do."

It had been some time, but I was pretty sure I knew what was supposed to come next, and I was pretty sure I wanted it to happen. I leaned a little closer. "Well, then get to work, Sheriff."

He pressed his mouth to mine, and I let out a little sigh. His lips were strong, and firm, and he reached up to stroke the side of my head right behind my ear. I opened my mouth and felt his tongue slide between my lips, probing gently, dancing across my teeth just long enough to be promising, then pull back. We parted, and he gave me a look that melted me right down to my core.

"Enjoy that bubble bath. And that trashy romance novel," he said, his lips just inches from mine. Then he pressed them to me again, this time more chaste, but still strong, passionate. I sighed again, like some silly girl in a Nicholas Sparks movie, but I couldn't stop myself. The firm lips, the strong hand on my face, the stubble scraping my cheek as he moved forward to whisper, "It's gonna take me a long time to sleep tonight." All that combined to make me real glad I was sitting in my truck and not trying to stand because that man made me weak in the knees like nobody in a very long time.

I gave him one last peck on the lips. "I had a lovely time, Willis. We'll have to do it again. Real soon." Then I cranked the put the truck in reverse and got the hell away from that man before I jumped his bones right there in Sharky's parking lot.

Jenny was sitting on my porch when I got home, on the two-seater swing next to Sheriff Johnny, both of them grinning at me like damn Cheshire cats. "Don't say a word, young lady," I warned as I walked up the steps and unlocked my front door. "I am allowed to go to dinner with a man if I want to, and I am allowed to kiss him if I want to."

"Did you want to?" Jenny asked, her voice sing-songy as she kicked her feet on the motionless swing. I was glad it wasn't moving. I had enough trouble with the folks on my street without my porch swing moving all by itself on a night with no breeze at all.

I felt a slight blush creep up my neck and across my cheeks as I very carefully did *not* look at the ghost. "I did. Want to, that is."

"So did you?" Jenny asked.

"I don't know that I feel the need to tell you that. A woman deserves to have some secrets, after all." I smiled as I pushed the door open.

"You might as well tell me. If you don't, I'll just go over to the cemetery and ask the Three Musketeers."

I laughed in spite of trying to act mad at her being all nosy. "Is that what you're calling those women? The Three Musketeers?"

"Well, it sounds a whole lot nicer than the Three Stooges," Jenny said, a little defensiveness creeping into her tone.

"Oh no, honey, don't get me wrong, I think it's fine. It's just that's what they called themselves when they were alive, and I think it's funny that's what you came up with to call them after death, without knowing it before."

"Oh," she said, mollified. "Okay, then. As long as you weren't making fun of me."

"Perish the thought," I said.

"Well, did you?" she persisted.

"Make fun of you?" I asked. "Maybe a little, but—"

"No, silly! Did you *kiss* him?" She barreled right past me into the living room and stared at me, then her eyes got big and she froze. "Somebody was here."

I didn't take another step into the house. "Are they gone?" I whispered, moving back out the door, trying hard not to make any noise.

"Yeah, they're gone now," she said.

"You're sure?"

"Yeah. There's nobody here but us. I can kinda...sense, I guess, living people now. I can feel them. Y'all, I mean."

That was new to me. I hadn't heard of spirits being able to sense the presence of the living. It kinda made sense, I reckon, since there are some living people who can feel ghosts when they're around. "And you're sure nobody is in there?"

"No, nobody's nearby but you. I can feel Mr. Martin in his bedroom next door, and Mrs. Cline over on the other side. I can even kinda feel the Jenkins kids home alone on the other side of Mrs. Cline, but that's all."

"Johnny, can you do that?" I asked. He was standing behind me, looking worried. He shook his head. I wasn't too surprised by that. I learned a long time ago that ghosts have different abilities. Johnny can't talk, and Jenny can. Both of them can move around freely, while some ghosts are stuck near a specific place. That sort of thing.

I turned back to Jenny. "How can you tell somebody was here if they've already left? Do people leave some kind of psychic residue behind?"

She looked at me, confused for a minute, then laughed. "Oh! No, there's a busted pane of glass in your back door and a muddy footprint in the dining room. I saw it, that's all."

"Dammit!" I said, stomping into the house, flipping on every light I passed. Sure enough, broken glass lay scattered all over the floor of my mud room, and there were several muddy footprints on my linoleum. "I just mopped this yesterday, now some son of a bitch had to come in here and make a damn mess."

"Miss Lila Grace, do you really think that's what you oughta be upset about right now?" Jenny asked. I turned and saw Sheriff Johnny flitting from room to room behind her. He walked over to us, held up his hands in a helpless gesture, and shrugged.

"Nothing's missing?" I asked.

Johnny shook his head.

"So something *is* missing?"

He shook his head again.

"Hold up one finger if you can't see anything missing, two fingers if you can." Sometimes working with a mute dead law enforcement officer is downright exasperating.

Johnny held up one finger. It is a mark of the level of gentleman that his mother raised that he used his index finger instead of a more demonstrative digit.

"So somebody broke in here just to…what? Track mud all over my kitchen? Hell, they could have waited until morning and come to the front door. Really piss me off and track dirt across the carpets."

"I think they were looking for this stuff," Jenny said. She stood at the dining room table, looking over the notes I had written from my interviews and the crime scenes. I walked over to join her and picked up one of the yellow legal pads I kept all my thoughts and theories on.

"What makes you say that, Jenny?" I asked. I saw Johnny standing behind the girl nodding, so obviously he thought the same thing.

"Everything is a little too neat. You left things kinda lying all scattered around because you knew wasn't nobody but you going to need to use the table. But now everything is in neat stacks, with everything perfectly straight."

I took another look at the table. With the exception of the legal pad I'd just laid down, she was right. Everything was at perfect ninety-degree angles, and every pile was now a neat stack. I looked a little closer, and all the stacks were organized by type of information, too. Interviews were in one stack, crime scene notes in another, stuff I thought of while talking to Jenny in another. Whoever went through my things left my house in better shape than they found it, except for the broken glass.

"Well, shit," I said.

"What's wrong?" Jenny asked. "I mean, besides the obvious."

"Now I have to call Willis. And I was going to make him call me."

CHAPTER 17

Willis came back through the house, his gun holstered, to where I sat on the front porch swing with Jenny. "The place is empty," he said, turning the rocker sideways and sitting down to face me.

"I told you that," I said. "Jenny did a thorough job of checking the place out before she'd even let me go get Daddy's gun and walk through the whole house myself." I reached out and patted the ancient twelve-gauge leaning against the wall beside me. Daddy's old gun had seen a lot of use when he was a younger man, bringing home dinner more than once when deer was in season. Since he passed, it mostly got used to scare crows out of the pecan tree in the back yard, or to take care of the occasional copperhead in the summer. I keep it loaded, though, with a shell of birdshot in first, then four shells full of double-ought buckshot just in case somebody's stupid enough to still be in my way after I dump a bunch of pellets into their behind.

"How did you know someone had been inside your house, Ms. Carter?"

"I'm Ms. Carter, now?" I asked with a smile.

"Well, I am conducting an investigation. But it could be that we might get a little less formal once my questions get answered. But not before. So, how did you know someone had been in your house?"

"It was too clean," I said.

"So someone broke into your house and...cleaned up?" Willis Dunleavy gave me almost exactly the same look he gave me the first time we met, when I told him I had a gift for talking to dead people.

"The stuff on the dining room table had been straightened. I left it all in big piles, but when I came back, it was all straight. And then there's the busted window on the back porch."

"Yeah, that's kind of a dead giveaway," he agreed.

"Plus, Jenny felt somebody's presence," I added.

The sheriff's pen stopped moving, and he looked up at me. "Now, you see, that's the kind of thing I can't put in my report."

"I can't possibly see how that's my problem, Willis," I said with a smile. "It's the truth. I know it, you know, and poor old dead Sheriff Johnny standing behind you knows it."

He jumped up and turned around like his butt was spring-loaded. I reared back in the swing, laughing fit to beat the band, and he just turned back around and sat back down in the chair in a huff. "I'm sorry, Sheriff," I said, still laughing a little bit. "Johnny ain't behind you. He wandered off after I called you, and I ain't seen him in half an hour. I was just pulling your leg."

"That's not funny, Lila Grace," he grumped, but I saw a little hint of a smile.

"Oh, don't be an old fuddy-duddy, Willis. If you can't laugh about the dead people that won't leave you alone, what in the world can you laugh about?"

"You are a very strange woman, Lila Grace Carter," he said, flipping his little notebook closed.

"You have no idea, Willis Dunleavy," I said, standing up.

He stood, and all of a sudden, we were standing on my porch, very close to each other, almost face to face. I felt his breath on my face, warm in the slightest chill of the evening air, and felt a warmth build inside me to match it.

"Well—" he started

"Would you—" I started at the same time, then stopped. "Go ahead," I said.

"No, you." He waved a hand.

I took a deep breath to quiet the butterflies in my stomach. "Would you like to come in for a drink?"

"That would be nice," he replied.

"I don't have anything but Jim Beam, and I don't keep much in the way of mixers," I said as I stepped past him into my den. I flipped off the porch light, as much to deter my neighbors from staring at my house as to keep the mosquitoes away.

"That's fine," he said, following me close, almost close enough for me to feel that hot breath again on the back of my neck. I slowed down a little, let him get closer. I could smell him, the warm man-smells of him. He smelled like leather from his gun belt, oil from his gun, and a hint of aftershave left over from the morning. Or maybe he splashed a tiny bit on before he came to my house? Either way, he smelled good. Strong, like a man should smell.

He pushed the front door closed behind us, and I heard him *click* the lock. I wove my way past the recliner in the den, past the dining room table with all my notes stacked too neatly on my grandmother's quilt that I repurposed for a tablecloth a few years ago, and walked into the kitchen. I got two jelly jars down out of the cabinet and put a few ice cubes in each one. I turned to walk back to the dining room but stopped when I almost bumped right into Willis, filling the door frame with my three-quarters full Jim Beam bottle in his hand.

"Sit down over there," he pointed to my ancient Formica-topped kitchen table. I did as he said and set the two glasses on the table. He put the bottle down in front of me, then turned and walked out the back door onto the small back porch/mud room where my washer and dryer, deep freezer, and tool boxes sat.

"What are you doing, Willis?" I called after him.

"I'll be back in a minute," he said. "Just pour the whiskey."

I gave a little shrug and did as I was told, content for the moment to let him have his little secret. Until I hear a horrendous banging coming from my back porch, that is. Then I shot up like a rocket myself and hustled to the door to see what the hell he was doing.

What he was doing was nailing a little piece of cardboard over the hole in my back door. He turned to me and gave me a sheepish little grin. "It won't keep out anything more determined than a wasp, but at least you won't have bugs getting in all night."

"Thank you, Willis, I appreciate it. You didn't have to do that, though. I wasn't going to make you work for your drink." *At least not that way*, I thought.

He smiled and put the hammer aside. "I don't mind. I don't get much chance to do things with my hands except shoot nowadays. I kinda miss it."

I stepped forward and stood up on tiptoes to kiss him on his rough cheek, enjoying the feel of his salt-and-pepper stubble on my lips. "Well, thank you, kind sir. Here is your reward." I kissed his cheek again and handed him a glass with three ice cubes and two fingers of whiskey in it. Then I turned and walked back into the kitchen and sat down at the table. I was pretty confident he'd follow, but I'll admit to a warm feeling in my belly when I heard his boots creak onto the linoleum.

"I dusted the knob for prints, but there was nothing but smudges. Not even your prints, which tells me either you wipe down your house every day, or the burglar wore gloves and took measures to make sure he wasn't discovered," he said, pulling out his chair and sitting down across from me, taking a slow sip of his drink.

I took a drink of my own, hearing the light tinkle of ice cubes shaking against the sides of my glass. I hated that noise because I wasn't rattling the ice around on purpose—my hands just wouldn't quite hold still. "Do you think it was the killer?" I asked. My voice sounded strange to my ears. It was a light, querulous thing, not the voice of a strong woman who lived on her own most of her life. It was the voice of a scared, delicate thing who needed protecting. I hated that voice a little bit and knocked back the rest of my whiskey to drown that simpering wretch.

Willis raised an eyebrow as I refilled my glass, but I didn't respond.

He took another sip and replied. "I can't imagine it would be anyone else. Just about everybody in town knows you're working this case in one way or another, and if they don't know it directly, they could probably figure it out from seeing us together in Sharky's twice in one day."

"Yes, I don't expect they would think much of my chances in the dating pool, so the logical assumption would be that we are working together." I heard the bitterness in my voice and tried to tell myself it was the whiskey talking, not the decades of sidelong glances from my neighbors, who were quick enough to knock on my door when they needed something, but had an alarming tendency to find something pressing on the other side of the street when they saw me on the sidewalk otherwise.

"I think your chances of landing a lawman are pretty good, if you ask me," Willis said. "And I don't mean Jeff."

We both laughed out loud at that. Willis, because he probably thought Jeff just another hapless yokel, and me because I would always see him as the sweet but slightly dim boy in my Sunday School class. "No, I don't think I'll be having a steak dinner with Jeff any time soon. He's sweet, but he's a little young for me."

"But you don't have a problem dating a cop?" Willis asked, leaning forward with his elbows on the table. His gaze became suddenly intense, and I thought for a second that I could see myself reflected in his deep brown eyes.

It took me a long moment to find my voice, but finally I said, "No. I think dating an officer of the law might even be a little bit…exciting." I let the last word linger, a little tease in the air. It had been a long time since I played this game, and I was rusty, but it was much more fun than I remembered. Maybe that's because I'd only played it with boys before, and this time I was fencing with a grown man. A very grown man.

I straightened up suddenly as Sheriff Johnny walked through the back door. He didn't open it, of course. He literally walked *through* my back door, making not the slightest sound to tell Willis that his predecessor had entered the room.

"What is it?" Willis said when I sat up. His cop instincts were on point, and he was on his feet with his gun out in an instant. He spun around to follow my gaze, but, of course, he saw nothing. He was face-to-face with Sheriff Johnny, who just stood there looking Willis up and down like he was some kind of interloper poking his badge in where he didn't belong.

"It's Johnny," I said, holding up my hands in a calming gesture. "He just came in through the back door, and he's motioning like he wants us to follow him outside." I stood up, and the room wobbled just a little bit. Drinks with dinner, a nightcap after, and now a strong drink in my kitchen amounted to more than my normal intake of liquor, and I was feeling the effects. It made Johnny less distinct, harder to see, and, thus, harder to understand.

Alcohol dulls my sensitivity, which is why I spent the month after my mother died drunk as a skunk. I didn't want to see her ghost; I just wanted to miss her like a normal person. Like every daughter who loses a mother, there were things between us that had been better left unsaid. And just like every strong-willed woman who came from a strong-willed woman, nothing remained unsaid between us. So, when she died, I crawled inside a bottle of Seagram's gin and didn't crawl out until I had it on good authority that she was no longer hanging around my house or hers. I haven't had a sip of gin since. Nowadays the mere smell of it makes me sick to my stomach.

I got hold of my equilibrium and followed Johnny out the back door and down the concrete steps. I opened the door, a concession to my physical form that Johnny still didn't have to make. I was also apparently going to have to have a conversation with him about making concessions to my privacy because if things moved the way I hoped with Willis, it certainly would not do to have a dead sheriff wandering into my home unannounced. I have enough issues with intimacy without turning my love life into a spectator sport, thank you.

CHAPTER 18

The three of us descended my back steps out into the small fenced in yard. Johnny floated straight off toward the back of the yard, past my four lone tomato plants, which still produced more of the red fruit than any five people could ever eat, much less just me. He walked through the laundry I hung out that morning before I started my investigation and went straight to the back fence.

We followed the ghost; Willis holding his pistol in his right hand and a small flashlight in his left. He didn't do that funny cross grip like the police on TV, he just kept his gun pointed at the ground with his finger off the trigger and aimed the flashlight at the ground in front of us.

I held up my hand when Johnny stopped and floated over one specific spot in my yard. I directed Willis's flashlight to the spot, and it illuminated an almost perfect men's boot print in one of the few spots devoid of grass in my yard. Maybe we had caught a break after all.

"This is good, Lila Grace," Willis said, pulling out his phone and wallet. He took a dollar bill from his wallet and laid it on the ground next to the footprint.

"You know Johnny's dead, right?" I asked. "You don't have to give him a tip."

"The dollar is for scale," he said. "It's an old trick to get a photo with a size locked in when you don't have your crime scene kit with you." He took a few shots with his phone, with and without flash, then picked up the dollar and put it back in his wallet.

"Stay here, but don't touch anything, including the fence right there," he said, all cop. "I'll be back in a minute with the good camera and my kit. Maybe we can catch another break and he left a print on the fence."

I cast a dubious look at the split rail fence along my back yard, thinking it was going to be a cold day in hell before we got a finger-print off the rough wooden surface, but I kept my doubts to myself. I watched the new sheriff walk around the side of my house, admiring the view as he went. The man definitely filled out a pair of blue jeans.

I turned to the former sheriff, who still stood beside me at the fence. "Thank you, Johnny. This could be just what we need to catch whoever hurt those girls."

He nodded. He knew exactly what a clue like this could mean, of course, as long as he'd been in law enforcement. We waited by the print for Sheriff Dunleavy to return, and he came around the side of the house moments later carrying a big toolbox in one hand with a camera bag slung across the opposite shoulder.

He set the toolbox on the ground and the camera bag beside it. First, he opened the toolbox and pulled out a small LED light on a stand, which he aimed at the print. Next, he pulled a big, professional-looking camera out and started snapping pictures of the footprint and the surrounding area. He pulled a ruler out of the toolbox and laid it on the ground next to the print, getting a more precise measurement than his dollar bill trick. Next, he pulled out two jars and a small Dixie paper cup, poured something from each jar into the Dixie cup, and stirred it with a tongue depressor, then poured a white mixture into the print.

"What is that, some kind of plaster?" I asked.

"Kinda," he said, not looking up from his pouring. "It makes a malleable rubber cast of the print and will also pick up any loose dirt from the impression, along with any trace evidence that was left behind from our visitor's shoe." When the footprint was filled with a thin layer of the white substance, he stood up and pulled out his flashlight again.

"While that dries, I'll see if there is any other evidence our friend left for us to find," he said, all business now that he was back on the job.

"Can I do anything to help?" I asked.

"You can hold the light while I take pictures," he said, passing me the big Maglite. I took it, and he put the camera around his neck. I followed as he walked toward the fence, careful not to take the most direct line to the print from the low point of the fence, but to walk beside the natural path. I pointed the light where he told me, and he snapped photos as we walked.

"I don't see anything," he said. "But in the low light, it's easy to miss something. I'll put the pictures on the big monitor when I get back to the office, and if there's something that will point us in the direction of a suspect, I'll find it."

"You're going back to the office tonight?" I asked. I felt a little disappointed at that. It's not like I was planning on him staying over at my house, not at all. I just thought we were nice and relaxed, maybe our evening didn't need to end quite so soon.

"Yeah, as soon as that cast dries. I'll scan the boot print and run it through a database of manufacturers. We don't have everything catalogued, but if it's a boot by a major shoe company in the US, I bet we'll have it."

"You have a computer program with every shoe print made in the United States?" I felt a little like Big Brother was watching, and he had a foot fetish.

"Distributed in the US," he corrected. "Most shoes sold in America aren't made here. But yeah, the FBI created a shoe print database a few years ago, and local law enforcement can access it. It's not free, but there's grant money available. Besides, I didn't spend all our budget on that tank the National Guard wanted me to take off their hands, so we can afford to look up a couple of footprints."

"I will never understand how law enforcement works," I said.

"Be glad of that, Lila Grace. Aim that flashlight over here." He pointed at the fence, then frowned. "Yeah, I can't pull any prints off that. The surface is way too rough and uneven. Our guy probably wore gloves climbing over it, anyway. Wouldn't make sense to carry gloves through your back yard just to put them on at the door."

He crouched by the fence, going over every inch of it closely. I got down on one knee beside him, feeling the dew soak through the knee of my pants. My crouching days were over long ago, arthritis in my knees making it painful and a little middle-aged spread across the hips making my balance treacherous. The last thing I needed was to sprawl on my behind in the middle of a crime scene.

"Do you see anything?" I asked, keeping my voice low. I don't know why I felt the need to whisper, my lot was sizable and unless someone felt the need to be standing on the other side of the fence, they couldn't hear me if I spoke in my full voice. I guess it was the suspense of it all.

He turned to me, and as he did, I caught a whiff of the smell of him. Leather, gun oil, spicy aftershave, Jim Beam, and just a hint of sweat blended together to make me swoon a little. It had been a long time since I swooned, and I was out of practice, but I remembered what it felt like. I liked it. I was also very glad I wasn't trying to maintain my balance because I would certainly have plopped down on my butt in the wet grass, a mood-killer if there ever was one.

"No, there's nothing here," he said, his voice low like mine.

I didn't feel like I needed to argue with him right then, but he was wrong. There was very definitely *something* there. I wasn't sure what it was, but I was very interested in finding out.

He stood up, and I followed suit. He packed up his tool kit and held out his hand. I stared at it, not knowing exactly what he wanted, then put my own hand in his. It felt good, the rough calluses of his palm against my own far-from-smooth hands. I work in my little garden too much to have very girly hands.

"While that's nice, Lila Grace, and I'm certainly not complaining about holding your hand, I need my flashlight back."

I was very glad it was too dark for him to see me blush. I let go of his hand and passed him the light, then turned and walked back into the house. We got to the living room, and I turned to the couch. "Are you...gonna stay a little while?" I felt tentative now, like we needed to figure out how to start all over again. He shuffled his feet, like a schoolboy trying to figure out whether to kiss the girl on the playground, pull her pigtails, or both.

"I better go ahead to the office and get these photos logged. Can't mess up the chain of evidence, you know."

I did. I knew he had an excuse to leave, so he would. Damn you, Sheriff Johnny, for finding clues! "I reckon I'll talk to you in the morning," I said.

"Yeah," he agreed. "Come on by the station around ten or eleven. I might have heard something about the shoe prints by then. We can figure out anything else we need to do then."

I stepped in to him, pressed my lips briefly to his, and then slipped back. His hands were full, and he was making his escape, so there wasn't going to be any kind of real goodnight kiss. "Good night, Sheriff."

"Good night, Lila Grace," he replied. "I'll call Jeff. He's on patrol tonight. I'll get him to make sure he gives your place a drive by every couple of hours to keep an eye on the place. If you need anything, you can call me direct. I'll be over here in a heartbeat."

I didn't bother exploring all the things I might call him in need of, not right at that moment. I just smiled and said, "Thank you."

We did that awkward dance of good nights and see you laters that people do when they aren't real sure where they stand with one another, then he was gone. I heard the trunk of his car close, then the big engine roared to life and disappeared down the street toward the police station.

I sat down on the couch, leaned my head back against my grandmother's throw pillows lined up across the back of the sofa, and let out of frustrated sigh. "Sweet Jesus, Lila Grace, why didn't you just jump the man? You are nothing but a horny old woman, and there is no way that fine piece of man is going to be interested in you," I said to the empty room.

As happens so often in my completely bizarre and slightly dysfunctional life, the empty room spoke back to me. This time in the voice of a dead teenager. "I don't know about that, Lila Grace. He seemed pretty damn interested to me."

"What would you know, child?" I asked. "You died a virgin." I clapped my hand over my mouth the second the words escaped and looked at Jenny, my eyes big as saucers. "Oh shit honey, I am so sorry."

The ghost child in my armchair gawked at me for a second, then laughed, throwing her head back and letting out a peal of pure joy and amusement. "Oh, good lord, Lila Grace, that's the funniest damn thing I've heard since I died!" She had another long laugh at my expense, then looked me in the eye. "First off, I was a cheerleader. Understanding what men want, both in high school and after, was kinda my thing. Second, I did *not* die a virgin, and thanks to me, neither will Alexander Zane."

"Alex Zane?" I asked. "Isn't he a sophomore at the University of South Carolina?"

"He is," Jenny confirmed. "But he wasn't two summers ago when he gave me a sob story about not wanting to go off to college a virgin when all his friends had lost their v-cards in high school. So we did it in the back of his daddy's old Suburban. He got pretty good at it before he went away to school, too." She gave a little smile at the memory.

"Do you think he could have…" I didn't quite ask the question, but I made it real clear what the question was.

Jenn thought for a few seconds, then shook her head. "Nah, we split up on good terms. Even got together a few times last summer when he was home. But we were never anything serious, and when he got a girlfriend this year, he called to tell me he couldn't see me over Christmas break. I think he expected me to be a lot more upset about it than I was. Which is to say, I wasn't upset at all. He was a nice guy, but I knew we were never going to be anything more than friends with benefits."

"Was there anybody else that might not have been so happy about breaking up with you as Alex?" I asked.

She looked a little offended, but she was the one who brought it up. "Well, I wasn't a slut, if that's what you're saying. I only ever slept with three boys. There was Alex, and Keith, my boyfriend right up until the end."

"That's two," I prodded.

"The other one was this boy I met at the beach last summer. I… kinda don't remember his name." This was a night full of firsts for me. I'd had my house broken into, made out with an officer of the law, and now I had a blushing ghost in my living room.

"That's okay, honey. We all have our wild oats to sow," I said.

"Did you?" she asked.

"Baby girl, I sowed entire fields when I was in college. But that was a long time ago. Now I'm going to go to bed and try real hard not to dream about sheriffs that smell good enough to slather in syrup and eat up like a stack of flapjacks."

CHAPTER 19

I woke up a little before the sun the next morning feeling almost more tired than when I went to bed. Just as I feared, good-smelling law enforcement officers dominated my dreams, and I tossed and turned all night. I stretched, listening my spine and hips crackling like a bowl of Rice Krispies, and shuffled off to the bathroom in my nightgown to take care of business.

A bracing cold shower later, I dressed in a pair of faded blue jeans and a worn Mast General Store sweatshirt that I picked up at the Goodwill in Spartanburg a couple of years back, and I meandered into the kitchen to fix up some breakfast.

"Well, it's about time you got up, lazybones," said the ghost sitting at my kitchen table. I stopped dead in the doorway and looked around. My kitchen could have been host of a busybody ghost convention, with Sheriff Johnny, Jenny, Helen, Frances, and Faye all crowded into one small room. It was a good thing they were incorporeal because otherwise it would have been awful crowded in there.

"Well, ain't you going to ask what we're all doing here?" continued Miss Faye, who was the sharpest-tongued sweet old lady I'd ever known, alive or dead.

"I ain't gonna do a damn thing until I've at least had a sip of coffee,"

I said, walking over to the counter. "Move, Johnny. You know I can only kinda see through you, and you're between me and my favorite mug."

He got out of the way, and I poured myself a cup of coffee into my favorite World's Best Grandma mug. I wasn't anybody's grandma, but it was an oversized mug and held almost two cups of coffee. Thank heavens I remembered to set the automatic coffee maker before I went to bed. I had a feeling I was going to need it with the damn United Nations of redneck ghosts floating around my house. I took a sip of the hot brown liquid, and between the shower, the coffee, and the adrenaline of being extra haunted at seven in the morning, my mind was almost clear by the time I took a seat at the table.

"Okay, folks, why are y'all here?" I asked.

"We did some looking around town last night after you went to bed," Miss Helen said.

"I helped," Jenny said, her face covered in a big grin.

"Yes, you did, darling. Now hush for a minute," Helen said, patting the girl's arm. I always found it interesting that ghosts could touch one another easily but had to expend a lot of energy to physically interact with anything in our world. Just another one of those "mysterious ways," I reckon.

"So we did a little digging, with Jenny's help, and we think we know who broke in your house yesterday," Helen said.

"Well, that's great," I said. "Because that might be the killer."

"That's what we thought, too," Miss Faye interjected.

I sat there, waiting, but no one spoke. "Well?" I asked. "Are y'all gonna tell me who it was, or should I just sit and wait for them to murder me, too?"

"You remember that freak Ian that Shelly hacked his phone? My dad told you about him," Jenny said.

I didn't, but it was early. I got up and went into the dining room. I got my little notebook and flipped it open to the pages where I wrote stuff down while I was talking to Mr. Miller. "Ian Vernon," I said. "He was the school newspaper's photographer. Shelly made it look like he sent dirty pictures to all his female classmates."

"That's the one," Jenny said, her face contorted in an ugly snarl. "He used to always take pictures of us at the football games, and he made sure to get the shots when we tossed a girl up in the air, or somebody was jumping around and her skirt would flip up. We all wore briefs, but it was still kinda skeevy."

"What makes you think he was the one who broke into my house?" I asked.

"I remembered that he always dressed like one of those freaks you see on the news that turns out to have a bomb in his locker or something, with long black coats and black boots and stuff. So I went and got Miss Frances, and she called the other women—"

"The Dead Old Ladies Detective Agency," Miss Helen corrected.

"She got the Agency together," Jenny said, then went on after a nod from Helen. "And we all went over to his house to look around."

"Jenny!" I said. "That's illegal. You can't just go into somebody's house without them asking you."

"What are they gonna do?" Jenny asked. "Arrest me? I'm dead. I think I've got other things to worry about other than getting arrested for breaking and entering."

"Besides, we didn't break," Miss Frances said. "We walked right through the walls into his bedroom. Nobody knew we were even there."

"Except that cat," Miss Faye said.

"Yeah, that cat didn't like us very much," Miss Helen agreed. "Just sat out on the hall meowing and hissing the whole time we were there."

"Are y'all going to tell me what you found, or just sit there congratulating one another?" I asked. I'm usually far more respectful of the dead, and of my elders, and certainly of anyone happens to be both, which account for four of the five people in my kitchen. But it was early. I blame my poor manners on lack of caffeine.

"The boots match," Miss Faye said. Her voice was typically matter-of-fact, like she was saying the sky was blue, or that grass was green. I whipped my head around to her so quick my brain had to take a second to catch up.

"The print we saw in Sheriff Dunleavy's camera matched the boots we found in Ian's closet perfectly," Jenny said. "That perv is definitely the one that killed me and Shelly." She folded her arms across her chest and looked at me, simultaneously proud of herself for finding the culprit and pissed off about being dead. I couldn't blame her. I kinda felt both those emotions right then, too.

"Well, I guess the next thing to do would be to call Sheriff Dunleavy and get him to interview Ian. Maybe we can find some reason to talk to him at school," I said.

"Isn't me telling you reason enough?" Jenny asked, her voice rising. I noticed the coffee cup rattling on the table in front of me, and I reached out to still the shaking porcelain.

"It is for me, honey, but I don't think your testimony is a whole lot of good in a court of law," I pointed out. Jenny scowled at me, but had no response. One benefit to being an old woman talking to young'uns is that sometimes they just shut up when they realize they're wrong. This does not happen nearly often enough with grownups.

I walked into the kitchen and picked up the cordless phone sitting on the antique icebox I used as a catch-all flat surface to hold the phone, phonebooks, notepads, ink pens, and bills that come in the mail until I get around to paying them. I walked over to my purse and dug out my cell phone, then shook my head and hung the cordless back up in its cradle.

"I reckon if I've got his number in my cell phone, I could just use that to call him, couldn't I?" I asked the air. Or I reckon I might have been asking the passel of dead people sitting in my dining room, but they ignored me, talking amongst themselves about all the "proof" they had that Ian was our murderer.

I pulled up Willis's number in my contacts list and pressed the button to call him, putting the phone on speaker so everyone could hear the conversation. It rang three times before he answered, and his voice was thick with sleep when he did. "Hello?"

"Willis? Sheriff?" I corrected myself, but not quite fast enough.

"Lila Grace?" He sounded like he was starting to come awake. "What time is it?"

I looked at the clock on the stove. "Seven-fifteen," I replied. "I'm sorry, I should have waited to call. I didn't even think that you might not be up yet. I just tend to get up early. I'm sorry, we can talk later. Give me a—"

"Lila Grace." His voice cracked over the lines. I stopped talking. "I'm awake now. What do you need? Did something else happen in the night?"

It took me a minute to figure out what he was asking. Of course, nothing else happened, he went *home*. Then I blushed a little at the direction my mind went, and I said, "No, no, nothing like that. But I think we might have caught a break in the case."

"What do you mean?" His voice had not a single trace of sleep-fuzzy in it now. I had his complete attention.

"The ladies went over to Ian Vernon's house last night, and they seem to think his boots match the print in my yard."

"The ladies? Lila Grace, you can't just go breaking into somebody's house on a hunch. Not only is that against the law, it's dangerous as hell. You know just about everybody around here has a shotgun. What if he'd shot you?"

"I think I'd be more worried about his daddy than Ian," I said. "From what I'm hearing, if Ian shoots anybody, it's with a camera. And I didn't go into his house. I didn't even know what they were doing until these crazy old biddies showed up in my kitchen this morning."

That got a glare from the assembled self-appointed detectives and a confused grunt from the man on the other end of the phone. "Lila Grace, what in the hell are you talking about?"

"Miss Helen, Miss Frances, and Miss Faye went over to Ian's house last night with Jenny. They walked through his bedroom walls and peeked at the bottom of his boots. Jenny says it's a perfect match for the boot print in the mud in my back yard."

"I say that because it is," Jenny said. "Tell him to arrest that little panty-snatcher!"

"Jenny also says that the boy is a little bit of peeping tom, trying to catch pictures up the cheerleaders' skirts," I added.

"Lila Grace, everybody from twelve to twenty spends half his life trying to get one glimpse of cheerleader drawers. I ain't arresting this boy on account of him being heterosexual. But I will go talk to Mr. Mitchell and see about getting an impression of the boy's shoes. If he wears those boots to school today, and his parents agree to it, and the school lets us, maybe we can get him to step in ink and walk on a sheet of paper for us."

"You don't have to talk to his parents," Jenny said. "He turned eighteen back in the summer. He got held back in seventh grade because he got the mumps and missed too many days." I relayed her words to the sheriff and got a sigh of relief.

"Well, that's one less bunch of asshats we have to deal with. I've already run into Ricky Vernon a time or two since I started. He's a real piece of work," Willis said.

"For somebody from out of town, you're catching on to life in the Upstate real quick, Sheriff," I said with a laugh. "You think Ricky's something, you should have met his granddaddy." Ulysses Vernon died when I was a little girl, but he made one serious impression the few times I met him. He was a huge man, with a long white beard that cascaded down over his overalls, completely covering up the t-shirt he wore. I never saw him wear shoes, even when he drove his old truck up to the house and dropped off a peach crate full of white liquor to my daddy.

Daddy would put cherries in that jar of liquor and let it sit on a shelf for about three weeks while he finished off Old Ulysses's last delivery, and about the time Daddy was out of liquor, the cherries had soaked into the moonshine and cut the taste just enough to make it drinkable. Daddy got a case of 'shine every two months from Ulysses until he drove his truck off the side of the road and wrapped it around a tree. Ricky took up the family business after his Granddaddy died, his own daddy having got killed in Vietnam, but the younger Vernon never had the nose for making liquor like his father did. I still got a case from Ricky every now and then, but half a dozen quart jars would last me almost a year, and I stuck cinnamon sticks in mine and let them dissolve all the way down before I drank the firewater.

"I'll meet you at the schoolhouse at nine-thirty. That oughta give me enough time to get some breakfast and get a shower. Then we can talk to young Mr. Vernon about his fascination with cheerleaders." Sheriff Dunleavy's voice jerked me out of my trip down memory lane, and I took a sip of coffee.

"I'll be there, Sheriff. Let's get this boy behind bars and find some justice for those girls." It all sounded so simple. But my life has never been simple.

CHAPTER 20

Nine forty-five saw us sitting in the principal's office with Mr. Robert Mitchell behind his desk and Ian Vernon slumped into a chair facing us. We were crammed into the little office like sardines, since the office was dominated by Mr. Mitchell's huge oak desk. I swear, you could have just about landed a helicopter on the thing, and it made me wonder what in the world he was trying to compensate for.

Robbie Mitchell had been the biggest hell-raiser in my Sunday School class for two years until his parents up and decided to switch to the ARP church and my life calmed down considerably. He never liked me much, since I didn't let him run wild like some other folks did, and I made him recite Bible verses every time he misbehaved. He had about memorized every word of Song of Solomon and Psalms before he changed churches. I reckoned if he'd stayed much longer, he probably would have gone to the seminary, and the world would have been deprived of a man with absolutely zero skill in education or administration, so naturally he went into exactly that field.

"Now Ian, you know that you can request your parents be here for this conversation," Mr. Mitchell said, but Sheriff Dunleavy held up a hand.

"Actually, Ian, according to these records—" He held up a file that I knew contained nothing but blank sheets of paper, since I had watched him pull them out of the copy machine in the main office and stick them into the folder. "According to these records, you're eighteen. That means you're legally an adult, and no, you cannot ask your mommy and daddy to be here when we're talking to you." Willis made it a point to make "mommy and daddy" sound as ridiculous and babyish as possible to keep the boy from asking for his parents.

"You can, however, ask for an attorney. Although, if you can't pay for one, you'll probably get a court-appointed lawyer from the ambulance chasers that hang out down by the emergency room," Willis added.

I knew this was a lie since there wasn't an emergency room for fifty miles, and there weren't any court-appointed lawyers in Lockhart. If the boy needed an attorney, they'd have to come from Union, or probably Spartanburg. That would take several hours to round one up and get over to the school.

"I ain't done nothing, so I don't need no lawyer," Ian said, his tone sullen and his words slurred. He looked everywhere around the room except at me, and I wondered why that would be. I didn't remember ever having any interaction with the boy, unless he maybe was with his father when he delivered my liquor once or twice. But his daddy delivered liquor to half to houses in town, so it's not like anybody cared.

"Then you won't mind if we ask you some questions?" Sheriff Dunleavy asked. He pulled out a small digital recorder and clicked it on.

"Nah, y'all go ahead. Ask whatever you want." Ian stayed slumped in his chair, working very hard to maintain his disaffected appearance. It wasn't working, at least not with me. His eyes kept sweeping the room, taking in every detail. He was paying very close attention to everything; he just wanted us to think he wasn't. I didn't know if that was the demeanor of a guilty person, or just a boy who doesn't want the adults to know he's scared.

"You understand that anything you say to the sheriff can land you in jail, don't you, Ian?" Mr. Mitchell asked, and I shot him a look that would have burned a hole right through his chest if I had anything like that super-hot vision that Superman throws around.

"Yeah, yeah," Ian said. "Like I said, I ain't done nothing, so won't be nothing."

I wasn't sure what that sentence meant, or even if it was really a sentence, but I ignored it and focused my attention on the boy's feet. Sure enough, they were clad in a pair of heavy black combat boots with thick rubber soles. I couldn't see enough of them to see if the treads looked anything like the boot print we found in my yard, but they were definitely a military-style boot.

"Where were you last night?" Willis asked, setting the recorder on Mr. Mitchell's desk.

"Home."

"When did you get home?"

"After school."

"Did you go anywhere between leaving school and home?"

"No."

I could tell the brusque answers were annoying Mr. Mitchell, and they were having a similar effect on me, but Willis seemed unfazed by them. I assumed that in his time working in the big city he'd found ways to get information from recalcitrant suspects.

"What if I said I don't believe you?" He leaned forward, dominating the skinny boy with his uniformed presence. Ian looked younger now, with the sheriff looming over him. His black jeans, black boots, and black t-shirt just made him look pale and nervous, not tall and intimidating like he certainly wanted. His spiky bright blond hair wavered a little as he shrank back from Willis's sudden invasion of his personal space.

"I'd say I don't give a shit what you believe because it's the truth." Ian jerked forward in the chair, almost nose to nose with the glowering sheriff.

Willis leaned back, a little smile tweaking the corner of his mouth. He got a rise out of the boy, got a full sentence out of him, which was some sort of progress. I enjoyed watching him work. He was good at this, working the push and pull of the boy's resistance.

"Have you ever been to Ms. Carter's home?" he asked.

Ian's eyes went wide, then his brow furrowed as he looked at me. "Her? Why would I go over to her house?"

"I don't know, Ian. Why don't you tell me why you went to her house?" Willis asked. I pushed down a smile as I saw what he was doing, getting the boy to admit to going to my house, then spinning that around to him being there last night.

"I didn't, man. I told you," Ian insisted. "Or if I did, I went there with my old man to drop off some liquor." He glared at Willis, all his hatred of authority restored in a blink. "Is that what this shit is about? You trying to use me to put the old man in jail? Shit, all you gotta do for that is ask. Yeah, he makes moonshine. Sells the shit out of it, too. Sells this old biddy a case whenever she calls, sells it to just about everybody in town. Except that asshole Sharky, he says Pop's liquor ain't good enough for his little pissant joint. Man, you want to get that old bastard on bootlegging, I'll tell you anything you want. You want to know about them half a dozen scraggly-ass weed plants he's got growing in the tool shed, too?" Ian leaned back, all smug viciousness at having turned coat on his father.

"We'll come back to all that," Willis said. I could see him mentally putting a pin in this point of the conversation. I knew from drinking with him at Gene's that he could care less about a little moonshining, but growing marijuana might be a whole different operation in his mind.

"I want to know why you were at Ms. Carter's place last night, poking around in her house. Why were you there, Ian?" Willis asked, his voice and eyes hard as flint.

"I wasn't, man! I done told you, I ain't never been there but to drop off liquor with Pops. What would I want in her house anyway? It ain't like she's rich or nothing." He got a crafty look on his face. "You ain't, are you?"

I almost laughed out loud at the clumsy boy, but managed to hold it in. "No, Ian," I replied. "I'm not rich. I have some antiques, but most of them are too big to move easily. You'd need a truck and help to get them out of the house. That's what makes this all the more confusing. Why would you break into my home?" I knew why, of course. I just wanted to keep him off-balance, to show him as few of my cards as possible.

"I didn't. I wouldn't. I ain't a thief. I ain't no kind of crook. I ain't no pervert, neither, no matter what them two dead bitches did to my phone. That's what this is about, ain't it? Y'all think since I hated them snotty bitches that I killed them. Well I didn't. I didn't break into nobody's house, and I didn't kill nobody. I'm a *good* person! I just…I just don't know how to talk to people sometimes, and sometimes people want to make out like I'm shit because my family's shit, and that pisses me off, 'cause I ain't nothing like them assholes, and then I get mad, and then they say that proves they was right all along, and… and…and…shit, I don't know. I just know I didn't break into nobody's house, and I didn't kill nobody."

He leaned back with his arms across his chest and a scowl on his face that only an aggrieved teenager can manage. I looked at Willis, but he didn't return my glance. He was studying the boy, all his attention focused on Ian's face, the set of his jaw, how he held his shoulders, whether his hands shook. He stared intently at the teen for several long moments, then leaned back abruptly, startling us both.

"Well, Ian, I reckon we can sort this all out real fast, if you'll agree to it," Willis said.

Ian cocked his head to one side, his distrust of Willis, all law enforcement, and everybody who could possibly be considered an adult evident in his face. "What you got in mind, Sheriff?"

"We took a photo and a mold of the boot print that the burglar at Ms. Carter's house wore. It was fresh, so we were able to get a very detailed impression. I'd like to compare that with your boots. If it's not a match, and those are the only boots you own, then you obviously didn't break into Ms. Carter's home." I noticed that he very carefully did not mention Jenny and Shelly's murders. It was one thing for him to throw away a burglary conviction, but if he mentioned anything about the boots in conjunction with the murders, and the shoes didn't match, we could have ourselves a regular O.J. trial down here.

"Well, shit, Sheriff, why didn't you just ask?" Ian said, leaning back in his chair and propping both feet up onto the table in front of him. My mouth fell open as I stared at the bottom of the boy's feet. He had apparently carved all the tread from the center section of his boots, then epoxied or glued somehow letters down the center of each foot. They looked like the brightly colored letter magnets that children play with, except on his right foot, it spelled out "P-I-S-S," and on the left foot, it read "O-F-F."

This was not the boot print of the person who walked through my back yard the night before. The boot print we had was normal, nondescript, and almost pristine. Ian's shoes were anything but. He was innocent, and he was our best lead.

"Are those the only boots you own, Ian?" Willis asked. I could read the disappointment in his every motion. His eyes were downcast, looking at his papers while the boy's grin burned a hole in the top of his head.

"Nah, I got another pair," Ian said with a smirk. Sheriff Dunleavy's head snapped up, then his shoulders sagged at Ian's next words. "I carved 'Suck It' on the bottom of them. Those are for the days when I'm feeling real bright and sunny. They don't get much wear."

Ian stood up and pushed his chair back under the table. "I guess I can go now, right? I've got lunch this period, and I'd really hate to miss it. It's fish stick day, and I can't wait to see what they're calling fish this week." He walked out of the office and slammed the door behind him.

Mr. Mitchell looked at Sheriff Dunleavy and me, his ears a little red from embarrassment. "Well, I suppose that didn't go quite as planned," he said, standing. He gestured to the door, and we walked out into the main office.

Mr. Mitchell walked us to the door of the main office, then said, in a voice pitched particularly for the student office monitors to hear, "I told you that Ian wasn't your burglar, Sheriff. You need to focus on catching real criminals instead of coming here and harassing my students. If you come back, you'd better have a warrant!"

Willis looked at him sideways for a minute, then nodded and walked out into the morning sun. I followed and held up my palm to Jenny as she drifted over. "Not now, honey, I need to go over to the Grill and get some pancakes with enough syrup to wash the taste of teenage jerk out of my mouth."

"I'll drive," Willis said. "I'm gonna need a whole lot of bacon to mask the taste of the crow I'll have to eat the next time I need anything from Mitchell." A disappointed sheriff, an embarrassed psychic, and a dead cheerleader headed off to breakfast. If that sounds like the beginning of a terrible joke, then you are beginning to understand how I felt. Like the beginning of a joke.

CHAPTER 21

We sat down at a table in the far corner of The Grill, the only restaurant in Maple Grove, and Willis nodded to most of the patrons. Everybody in the place recognized us, and there was more than one whispered conversation that started up as soon as we sat down.

"Do you want me to go listen to what they're saying?" Jenny asked, a gleam in her translucent eye. I had the distinct impression that child was enjoying this whole undead detective thing more than just about anything she'd enjoyed while she was alive.

I shook my head, looking at Willis, but talking to Jenny. "No, sweetie, there ain't no point. I can just about tell you what they're saying. Beth Shillington over there is telling her husband Harold that she heard I danced around nekkid in my back yard under the full moon to get my power to talk to dead people. Harold is gonna nod and tell her that he saw the two of us at Sharky's together yesterday. Then Beth is gonna get on him for going to Sharky's after she has done told him not to drink during the week on account of how much it cost them to get out of his last DUI."

I jerked my head at a table with half a dozen elderly women sitting by the window. "That over there is Helen's Sunday School class.

They'll be talking about how sinful it is for us to be dining together, an unmarried woman and man breaking bread being nothing but temptation to fornication and all." I very studiously did not look at Willis when I said "fornication," but I felt the tips of my ears get red anyway. "This despite the fact that three of those women are carrying on with unmarried men themselves, and two of them are sleeping, unbeknownst to the other, with the same man!"

Jenny burst out laughing so hard she almost fell through her chair, and Willis looked at me with his eyebrows up. "And how exactly did you come by this knowledge, Lila Grace?"

I just smiled at him. "Willis, darling, I'm the only living person those three old dead busybodies have to gossip to. Where in the world do you think I got the information?"

"I don't know, but can we revisit the idea of you dancing around nude under the full moon?" He smiled, and his grin only grew as I felt my cheeks flame.

"No, we cannot," I said, unrolling my napkin from around my silverware and placing it in my lap. "Unless you've got a bottle of Pappy Van Winkle stashed somewhere in your office. You come up with some top-shelf bourbon, Sheriff, and we can certainly have a conversation." I gave him what I hoped was a flirtatious smile, but it had been so long since I flirted I couldn't promise any level of proficiency with it.

Just then I was saved my Renee Walkin coming up to the table, her little notepad in hand. Renee was married to Phillip Walkin, who owned The Grill, and she was the chief waitress, hostess, silverware roller, floor sweeper, and doer of everything else that didn't involve the kitchen. Phillip ran the kitchen like he was a redneck Gordon Ramsey, and their son Phil Jr. was the dishwasher. I knew Renee and Phillip had high hopes for Junior taking over the place when they retired, but I'd never seen Phil Jr. aspire to anything more than catching enough fish to keep his belly full.

"Morning, Lila Grace, Sheriff," Renee said with a smile. She always had a kind word for me, ever since we were kids. She was a couple years behind me in school, and we were never real close, but she was one of the few people in town who never made fun of me or looked at me funny. I asked her about that one time, and she just said, "I was told to treat people like I wanted to be treated. I don't like it when people are mean to me, so I try not to be mean to other people." The world could use a few more Renees.

"Morning, Renee," I said. "Anything special today?"

"We got blueberry pancakes, but they ain't real good. I think the blueberries ain't quite ready yet. But I've got a few chocolate chip pancakes left if you want something sweet."

"I think I'll just do two eggs over medium, with bacon, grits, and one of them big old cat-head biscuits you got back there."

"I can do that," she said with a smile. "What about you, Sheriff?"

Willis looked at me like I was speaking French, then asked, "What in the world is a cat-head biscuit?"

Renee and I both laughed, drawing more nasty looks from the Sunday School biddies, and Jenny looked confused, too. "It just means it's a great big ol' biscuit, Sheriff. I don't use no biscuit cutter, so my biscuits always turn out too big, and not real round, so they look about the size and shape of a cat's head," Renee said.

"I assure you, Fluffy was not harmed in the making of Renee's biscuits," I added.

Willis smiled and said, "Then I'll have two eggs, scrambled, with double bacon, hash browns, and a biscuit. It can be the size of whatever animal you see fit." He gave Renee a warm smile to let her know he wasn't picking on her for talking country, and she walked off with a grin.

"I like her," he said. "She's funny."

"She's a good woman," I said. "She's done a good job raising her kids, and keeping Phillip in line. I swear, to know him growing up, you never would have thought that boy would turn out to amount to nothing."

"Why's that?" Jenny asked. Her face was a little glum, and I wasn't sure if it was because she wasn't going to grow up, or just because she had to sit there smelling all that good food and couldn't eat any of it.

"Well," I said. "He raised plenty of hell back in his day, wildcattin' around with the boys. He once wrecked two identical cars in the same curve on the same road, a year apart, driving like a bat out of hell on these back-country roads. I reckon if you would have asked me when I was twenty who I knew that was least likely to see thirty, it would have been Phillip Walkin. But here he is, a respected businessman, father, and I think he's a deacon over at the ARP church. Just goes to show you can't never tell."

"Yeah, I reckon not," Jenny said. She stood up and drifted off. "I'm going to go talk to the ladies at the cemetery and see if we can come up with anything else. I'll meet you back at the house later."

"Okay, honey. I'll see you in a little while," I said, still trying to look at Willis while I talked to her spirit.

"She okay?" Willis asked.

"I don't know. I know she was real disappointed when Ian turned out to be innocent. He was a good suspect, and if he turned out to be guilty, she could move on. I think she might be starting to feel the permanence of the whole thing."

"Death?"

"Yeah," I said. "Some spirits don't really get that it's forever at first. It takes some time, and when they do, they have to adjust to that. It's hard, especially if they were real active in life and had a lot going on, like Jenny did."

"She was real young, too," he added.

"Yeah, that can have something to do with it. I'm not sure it always does, but it can."

We finished our breakfast and left, Willis nodding to even more people on the way out. He dropped me by my truck back at the high school and headed to the police station to review crime scene photos and forensics from Shelly's car.

I went home and found Jenny and Sheriff Johnny sitting on my porch swing. I sat in the rocker beside them. "Hey, Jenny," I said.

"Hey." She didn't look at me.

"I reckon you're disappointed with how this morning turned out."

"Yeah." Monosyllabic answers was one of the reasons I was glad I never had teenagers, and why I stuck to teaching elementary school kids in Sunday School. I've never known how young'uns that will mouth off at the drop of a hat can become almost mute whenever you try to ask them a question.

"Well, we ain't giving up, sweetie. Ian was a good suspect. He had all the reasons in the world to hate y'all; he just didn't do it. But we'll figure out who did, I promise."

Sheriff Johnny's head snapped around to me, and he wiggled his fingers in the air. "I know, Johnny. I ain't supposed to make promises I don't know if I can keep. But I'm going to do everything I can to keep this one. This child has done made herself important to me, and I don't like the idea of disappointing her."

He nodded, and stood up, walking through the front door into my house. I sat there for a few seconds before he stuck his head and torso through the wall and waved at me to follow him.

"I swear, child, if I live to be a hundred, I will never get used to that."

Johnny wiggled his fingers at me, and I feigned anger at him. "No, Johnny, I am not already a hundred! Dammit, old man, if you don't quit wiggling them smartass fingers at me, I'll wiggle one back at you!" I got up and mock-stomped into the house, but I noticed Jenny cover her mouth to hide a giggle as I did.

Johnny was standing by the back door when I got to the kitchen, kinda looking around everything. "What do you see, Johnny?" I asked.

He shrugged. "Yeah, I don't see anything, either," I said.

He wiggled his fingers at me. "That is a little strange. You're right, there's *nothing* here. It ain't just like the guy who broke in wore gloves; it's like he didn't leave any smudged prints, or trace evidence or anything behind, just a little mud from your backyard. That's pretty good for a high school kid, ain't it?"

Johnny nodded, then made a sweeping arm motion around the kitchen. "Yeah, there ain't a speck of mud or nothing. And it ain't like I stayed up late to mop the kitchen, neither. Just swept up the broken glass in put it in Sheriff Dunleavy's evidence bags. But there wasn't a single scrap of dirt or fabric left behind. Whoever did this knew what they were about. This wasn't their first rodeo. I reckon I oughta go see if I can figure out what I've got in the dining room that was worth them breaking in here."

I went into the dining room and sat down in front of a stack of folders. These files were copies of all the crime scene photos and police reports from Jenny's basement, both visits, and from Shelly's car. I spent a solid three hours digging through those files, and didn't find much.

Both girls died of broken necks, which made sense for Jenny, since she got pushed down the stairs, but not as much for Shelly. Jenny's house showed no signs of forced entry, and so far, the police had no idea where Shelly was killed. The time in the water pretty much destroyed any trace evidence that might have been in Shelly's car, and the time that passed between her death and it being ruled a homicide meant that there was no real evidence available in Jenny's basement either. Whoever killed these girls was the worst kind of person—ruthless and smart.

CHAPTER 22

I was sitting at my dining room table, going over the pictures of Shelly's car for what felt like the twentieth time, when I heard a car pull up in front of my house. Heavy footsteps pounded up my steps, and there was a sharp knock on my door.

I walked to the front door, careful to keep an eye on the shotgun leaning against the wall, but relaxed when I recognized Willis's form through the curtains. I pulled open the door to find him standing there on my front stoop holding a brown paper bag and wearing a goofy grin.

"I brought lunch," he said, breezing right past me like he owned the place. "I figure if this morning pissed you off anything like it did me, you've been up to your eyeballs in case files all morning and didn't even realize it was two o'clock."

My stomach answered for me, letting out a noisy rumble at the smells coming from the sack he carried. "I'll get some tea. Come wash your hands and get some paper plates. The dining room table is covered up, so we'll eat in the kitchen."

He followed me through the dining room into the kitchen and set his bag down on the stove. I looked at my worn brown Tupperware tumblers and decided to use the good glasses, the ones made out of actual glass, for a change. Admittedly, they were old Smurfs glasses I got at the Hardee's drive-thru thirty years ago, but I thought they were at least a little upgrade from the Tupperware. Mama taught me to put my best foot forward, and I'm sure she was rolling over in her grave at the fact that my idea of putting my best foot forward was choosing the Smurf glasses over the Tupperware. My mama and I never were on the same page as far as my feminine wiles went.

Willis laughed as I walked to the table holding out the cartoon glasses. "I see we're using the good china."

"I don't scrimp when company comes," I replied. "Now don't give me no crap, or I'll make you drink out of a Solo cup."

"I don't mind a Solo cup. Now, I don't know what you like, so I just got a couple of sandwiches, and if there's one you don't like, I'll eat it."

"What did you bring?" I asked.

"I stopped by The Grill and got a couple of cheeseburgers, a BLT, and a barbecue sandwich, with two orders of French fries."

"That sounds great," I said, turning back to the fridge. I pulled out a couple of squeeze bottles of condiments, a jar of homemade sweet pickles, and some Duke's mayonnaise. Willis passed me a plate, and we spread out the sandwiches between us. We each took a burger and some fries, and I cut the barbecue sandwich in half and put one piece on my plate.

"I'll take the other piece," Willis said, holding out his hand. Our fingers brushed as I passed it to him, and I looked up to see his ears blushing. I ducked my head so he wouldn't see the flush on my own cheeks, silently kicking myself for acting like a nervous schoolgirl.

"Well, you're right," I said after I'd taken the edge off my hunger with half a cheeseburger and some fries. "I've been up to my eyeballs in case files all morning, and I don't have any more of a clue than I did when we walked out of the school."

"Me neither," he admitted. "I hoped we could talk through some things after lunch and maybe come up with something. Is Jenny around?"

"No, and I haven't seen Sheriff Johnny in a while, either. Jenny went over to the graveyard to talk to the Triplets, but I don't know where Johnny is."

"The Triplets?"

I explained about Helen, Faye, and Frances, and he laughed. "Yeah," he said. "They sound like three peas in a pod."

"Oh Lord, you ain't wrong. They were thick as thieves in life, and death hasn't made them like each other any less."

"That's kinda sweet, ain't it?" he asked, a thoughtful expression crossing his face.

I swallowed a mouthful of barbecue and asked, "What do you mean?"

"Well, here you've got three women who were such good friends in life that they're still spending all their time together even after they've passed. And you've got somebody like Sheriff Johnny, who loved his town so much that he wouldn't leave even after death. He still wants to keep an eye on things, even though he can't really do a whole lot about it now. It's nice, you know? Says a lot of good things about a place, that people care that much about it."

"I hadn't thought about it like that," I admitted. "I reckon when you spend your whole life seeing dead people and trying to help them move on, you don't stop to think too much about what would make somebody want to stay." I chewed my sandwich for a minute or two more in silence, then picked up my napkin from my lap and laid it across the plate.

"I surrender," I said. "If I eat another bite, I won't be good for nothing the rest of the day. Do you want to take that BLT back to the office? Eat it later?"

"I'll see if Jeff wants it, but he probably won't touch it. He's real particular about his food."

"Always has been," I said. "Even when he was little, he had to have the crusts cut off his bread, and the sandwiches cut into little triangles. He always wanted plates with dividers, so his food didn't touch. He's real particular about most everything."

Willis laughed. "God knows that's the truth. I borrowed a pen from his desk one day and you would have thought the world was gonna

end. I even walked over to the cabinet and handed him two to replace
it, but it wasn't the right pen. I haven't touched his desk since. Just
ain't worth upsetting the apple cart."

"His mama was like that, too. She was in charge of the bulletins at
church for the longest time, and they were always beautiful, but
heaven help you if they didn't get folded just right. I watched her rip a
deacon up on side and down the other one morning because he told
her it wasn't a big deal."

"I bet he didn't make that mistake again," Willis said, chuckling. He
stood up and put the spare sandwich in the paper bag and looked at
me. "Where's the trash can? I'll throw away the plates if you'll fix us a
couple more glasses of tea."

I pointed to the sink. "Under there. Drop the plates in there and
let's go to the dining room. Maybe together we can see something in
all this mess." I opened the freezer and dropped a few more ice cubes
in each glass, then topped off the tea and followed him into the dining
room. I passed him his Papa Smurf glass and set my Smurfette glass
down on a coaster.

"You got another one of those?"

"Smurfette glass? No, I just got the one set. I got Papa Smurf,
Smurfette, Brainy Smurf, and Gargamel and that cat of his."

"Azrael," he said. "But I meant a coaster."

"Oh!" I grabbed him a coaster and sat down behind the stack of
folders. "Where should we start?"

"Let's look at your suspect list compared to mine and see who I
have an alibi for already," he said. He leaned over and picked up a slim
black briefcase I never even noticed him set down on the floor. An
iPad and a portable keyboard appeared, and he looked up at me.

"Aren't we Mr. Technology?" I teased.

"I'm old, Lila Grace, but I ain't dumb. This thing is the best thing
that's happened to law enforcement since the bulletproof vest.
Camera, communication device, and all my case files right in one
place. I don't know how I caught any bad guys without it."

"Might have involved more running, old man," I said with a grin
and a poke to his belly.

"Hey!" he protested. "I'm a sheriff now, I don't have to run. I have people for that."

"You have Jeff for that," I corrected. "I've seen Jeff run. It looks like a cross between a very slow ostrich and a demented hippopotamus. That boy is a lot of things, but coordinated and athletic are not any of them."

He laughed and nodded. "Jeff is an invaluable asset to the department, but he ain't gonna win any forty-yard dashes, that's for sure. Now, who do you have on your list that still looks good to you?"

"Well, there are the girls that didn't make the cheerleading squad, but double homicide seems a bridge too far even for a heartbroken teenage girl, and I've seen some things in that regard."

Willis looked like he was about to say something, but shook his head like he was changing the topic and said, "We talked to all the girls who tried out the past two years and didn't make the squad. All but one of them had an alibi, and she was so tore up I can't imagine it was her. Turns out Jenny was actually working with her some weekends to get better so she could audition again next year."

"That definitely doesn't sound like anybody with enough of an axe to grind to murder someone," I said. "What about the kids from the church beach trip last year? Reverend Turner seems to think there may have been some alcohol involved, and possibly even..." I lowered my voice. "Sex."

The sheriff grinned but shook his head. "There were only half a dozen people on the trip in addition to Jenny and Shelly, and three of them were girls we'd already cleared. The three boys all have solid alibis. Turns out in a town this size, it's pretty easy to account for most everybody's whereabouts on a Friday night after a home football game."

"Most of the underage population is either in the parking lot of McDonald's, the parking lot of the high school, or over at the dam parking," I said.

"Some of them have started going out to the landfill now," he added.

"That's a new one on me, making out at the trash dump."

"The older section of the landfill is pretty nice. They've put down sod and landscaped it. I think the county is talking about building a golf course out there once they get one or two more sections filled up," Willis said.

"I think I'll stick to making out in the comfort of my own home, thank you."

"Is that an invitation, Ms. Carter?" he asked. "Because I have to remind you, I'm still on duty."

I smiled at him, enjoying the flirting. "Why, Sheriff, I thought you were on your lunch break." I batted my eyes at him, then laughed out loud at the flush that crept up his cheeks.

"Lila Grace, you might be the single most infuriating woman I have ever met, and I was married. Twice!" he spluttered, laughing a little.

"Twice, huh," I said.

"Yep," he said. "Three times, if you count being married to The Job, which both of my wives accused me of on more than one occasion."

"What happened?" I asked.

He sighed, then looked at me for a second, like he was making up his mind. "Well, I reckon we oughta go ahead and get this all out in the open. The first time I got married, I was twenty-two years old, full of piss and vinegar, and raring to arrest every bad guy in the world. Gina, that was my wife's name, was a great gal, good-looking, good cook, good job as a CPA for some high-rise accounting firm downtown."

"What happened?" I repeated.

He gave me one of those "I'm getting to that" looks that men get when you're trying to get them to talk about something they don't want to talk about, usually their feelings on something deeper than football.

"She got pregnant and wanted me to leave the force. Said she couldn't see herself raising a kid not knowing if I was going to walk through the door at the end of my shift or not. I didn't want to quit, but she was dead set on it, so I filled out the paperwork. I was going to work security in the building where she worked, getting fat and watching security cameras."

"But that didn't happen," I said.

"No, that didn't happen. She lost the baby, and there were complications from the miscarriage that made her unable to get pregnant again. I stayed home with her for a week, then she practically pushed me out the front door to go back to work." He looked at me with a sheepish grin. "I'm not real good at sitting still now, and this was thirty years ago. You can imagine what I was like then."

"I'd rather not," I said with a smile so he knew I was just teasing.

"So I went back to work, and after another week or so, she went back to work, and we settled back into our everyday lives. Then one day I come home and she's standing in the kitchen with my paperwork to leave the force in her hand. She starts screaming at me about why I haven't put in my notice yet, and how I don't care about her if I'm going to keep putting my life in danger, and all this stuff about how me being a cop is selfish, and I'm just standing there with my mouth hanging open like a trout laying on a dock."

He took a deep breath, then dove back in. "When she lost the baby, all the thoughts of leaving police work went out of my head. To me, that was the only reason I was quitting, and now that we weren't going to have a kid, I figured I'd just be a cop the rest of my life. But to her, me leaving the force was more about her feelings and a lot less about the kid thing."

"I see both sides," I said, not wanting to step on his fragile ego and tell him that he was an idiot. He probably already had that much figured out.

"Yeah, and I was a kid, too. I'd see things a lot differently now, but back then, I could barely see past the end of my own nose. So we had a huge fight, and she threw me out. Told me I had to choose being a cop or being married, that I couldn't be both. And, being stupid, and stubborn, and twenty-six, I became another statistic about cop marriages."

"I'm sorry," I said. "But at least you had her for a little while." I didn't mean to throw that out there. Didn't mean to make it about me, but the look of pity that flashed across his face for just a second told me that's exactly what I'd done.

"Yeah, I had a couple of good years with her, and a few really bad months, but all in all, it turned out for the best in the end. She married a guy who moved up to become the CFO of that company she worked for, and she quit working at thirty-five to take care of three adopted kids and do charity work. We haven't spoken in years, but I get a Christmas card every year."

"That's nice," I said. "At least it ended up good. What about your second wife?"

His face darkened, and I knew that we'd crossed into a topic he wasn't very comfortable with. "That's a much uglier story. Are you sure you want to hear it?"

His words were telling me to say no, but his eyes told the story of a man who really needed to talk. I leaned forward, put my hand over his, and said, "Talk to me, Willis."

CHAPTER 23

He smiled across at me, his brown eyes squinting a little. It was a slow smile that started at his eyes and flowed down like molasses, but never grew very big. "It's not a huge tragedy, Lila Grace, don't worry. I'm not so noble as to have sat by her bedside for a year while she slowly withered from cancer or anything like that. No, it's a boring story with a few exciting moments, but there's unfortunately nothing unusual or even uncommon about it."

I didn't speak, just held on to his hand and kept looking at his face.

"Okay, fine," he said after the pause grew to uncomfortable lengths. "Nancy and I were both married before, and both divorced when we met. It was one of those rare things—we met as adults not in a bar, not as a hookup from friends, and not in a church."

"Where did you meet, then?" I asked. He'd hit the top three places I knew of that grown-ups met, so I was genuinely curious.

"Waiting in the lobby of an oil change place. I was getting my cruiser worked on, and she was getting the brakes checked before a road trip. I needed new windshield wipers, and she turned out to need new brake pads, so we started talking. I ended up sticking around an extra hour after my car was done, just to talk to her."

"That's sweet," I said.

"Yeah, well, she was easy to talk to, and easy on the eyes. I reckon back then I probably wasn't too bad to look at myself. I was a good forty pounds lighter, with a little more hair on top, and a lot less hair in my ears."

"You're not doing too bad for an old man, Willis," I told him, patting his hand.

"Flattery will get you pretty much anywhere you want to go, pretty lady," he replied, and I felt the blush creep up my chest to my neck. I looked away from his eyes for a second, and he resumed his story. "So we went out a few times, and after a little while, we decided that we liked each other more than casually. She wasn't crazy about the idea of marrying a cop, but I'd made detective by then, so I wasn't walking a beat anymore. At least I worked hard to convince her that was safer, anyway."

"We dated for about a year before we got married, and were married for a good eight years." He chuckled. "I usually tell people I was married for six good years, and two lousy ones, but that's not fair to Nancy. She was great to me, right up until the time it all fell apart. I wasn't as great to her, though."

"What happened?" I asked.

"Same thing that happened with Gina. Same thing that happens to most cops, I guess. At least from talk around the stations, anyway. I got promoted to homicide, started spending more and more time out at night, at crime scenes and dealing with informants, suspects, and other unsavory types. It made me a darker man, and I was never exactly the life of the party. After a while, I wasn't the man she married anymore, so…"

"So…what?" I asked. "You've got to remember, I'm the old spinster. I've never been married, to a cop or to anyone else, so I don't know what 'so…' means."

"She cheated," he said bluntly. My eyes snapped up to his face, and I could tell by the set of his jaw and the flat gaze he directed at the table that it still hurt him to the core, even now. "She cheated, with a guy from her work. A middle manager named Rico, who was in good shape, used a lot of hair product, and pay her a lot of attention."

I eyeballed the buzzed gray stubble sticking out maybe a quarter-inch from his head. "I can see how you would lose out in the hair product department."

Willis laughed, a genuine laugh with just the lightest hint of self-deprecation behind it. "Yeah, I didn't do a lot of that kind of stuff even back before I started going thin on top. Once I hit thirty-five, my hairline didn't recede, it went into full retreat."

I chuckled, and said, "That's funny, that's about the time my boobs started moving south for the winter and never came back north." We both laughed with the ease that only people who have grown into being comfortable with themselves can have.

His smile faded away, and he said, "There's more. Because when you have a man in his late thirties, who's spent a life in law enforcement, and he finds out that his wife is unfaithful, you have one of three possible outcomes. Way too often, it ends up with the cop knocking his wife around. Well, the only redeeming quality I held onto in this mess is I never hit Nancy, or any other woman that wasn't actively trying to kill me."

I filed that away for future investigation because I thought there was a little too much specificity in that sentence to not have an interesting story buried in there somewhere, but I kept my mouth shut. I just sat there, waiting for the rest of his moment of confession.

"It's pretty obvious from the fact that I'm sitting here that I didn't swallow the barrel of my service weapon, although I'll admit I thought about it more than once. This whole scene cost me years of therapy."

"So that means you did exercise Option Number Three?" I asked.

"Yep," he nodded.

"Which is what, exactly?"

"I waited outside their work, followed them to a motel where they met up to have sex, and when they went into the room, I waited about fifteen minutes, then knocked on the door."

"Oh no," I said.

"Oh yeah. Rico came to the door, and I broke his nose with it. I shoved the door into his face, then shoved my way into the room. I beat the shit out of him with my wife naked and screaming the whole time. I broke his nose, three ribs, his collarbone, one arm, and three bones in my right hand. I went full crazy on his ass. I'm not anywhere close to proud of it, but it happened, and I've got to carry it with me."

"What happened after that?" I asked. I wasn't sure I wanted to know the whole sordid story, but he seemed like he needed to get it all out, so I figured I'd better let him lance the whole thing, as it were.

"I sat down in the one chair in the room—you know how those cheap motel rooms are set up, with a little crappy table by the window and one chair over there. Well, I sat down in that chair and just stared at Nancy. She was scared, and I couldn't blame her. I figured she would be, that's why I made it a point to leave my gun in the car."

"I sat there for a minute, then she called the cops. I didn't go anywhere, but I did tell her she might want to think about putting some clothes on before they got there. She wore a sheet into the bathroom and came out about the same time the first patrol car got there. I was still sitting at the table, my badge out in front of me, both hands in plain sight. Rico had managed to sit up and had his back to the dresser, a towel over his junk, and another one pressed to his bleeding nose. He was spouting all kinds of crap about suing me and making sure I spent the rest of my life in jail, but it was all crap."

"What do you mean?" I asked.

"I'm a big dumb ox sometimes, Lila Grace, but I ain't stupid. I knew going in there how everything was going to play out, and it went just about how I expected it to. I got busted back down to a patrolman, spent a month suspended without pay, and ended up giving Nancy pretty much anything she wanted in the divorce. She got the house, both cars, and all our savings. I got to keep five grand in our bank accounts, my clothes, and my bass boat. I had to borrow a truck from a friend to tow the boat out of our driveway so I could sell it for enough money to buy a beat-up Saturn.

"But I didn't serve any time. I knew the cops that came to arrest me. I went through the academy with one of them, and I'd met the other one a few times at union meetings. They didn't hassle me much, and I didn't give them any crap. The DA didn't push too much, and Rico couldn't get them to press anything more than assault charges. Intent wouldn't stick because I left my gun in the car, so I obviously didn't want to kill him. I paid a fine and did community service for that, and the whole thing was behind me. I haven't seen Nancy since we met in the lawyer's office to finalize our divorce. She sold the house and moved to Phoenix, and I decided that I'm pretty much not the marrying type."

"I don't know that I think that's very fair, Willis," I said. "But if that demotion is one of the things that kept you from getting a job in a bigger city, I can't say as how I don't like it at least a little bit."

He smiled at me, a shy little thing that kinda danced around the corners of his mouth and eyes for a few seconds, then ran away when it saw me looking. "I ain't proud of what I did, but I'd do it again. That little sumbitch needed an ass-whooping, and I reckon it was on me to deliver it."

"Is this where you go into some stupid diatribe about the man code?" I asked, taking a sip of my tea.

"No, this ain't got nothing to do with the man code," he said. "This is just about being a decent human being. Marriage is supposed to be sacred, and it ain't something to interfere with. I wasn't the best husband to Nancy, I know that. But I didn't deserve having that little snake come into my relationship with his good teeth and his hair gel and steal my woman away from me. It hurt my pride, probably more than it heart my heart. If I was to be honest about it, me and Nancy had been growing apart for a while, and it was almost something of a relief when we finally split up."

"But your pride demanded that you beat somebody up over it." I heard the disapproval in my voice, but I didn't mean it much. I grew up in a small town around men, and I knew them to be fragile creatures. The big idiots could cut a finger off with a chainsaw and keep going with it wrapped in duct tape, but God forbid you hurt their feelings.

"Yeah, it did," he sighed. "It ain't the stupidest thing I've ever done, but it makes the top five, that's for damn sure. Come to think of it, most of the rest of them involve a woman, too."

"Where does going out with a woman who talks to dead people rank?" I asked. My voice was softer than I wanted it to be, and the joking lilt I planned on being there was missing somehow.

He reached across the table and took my hand in his. "Lila Grace, I know you ain't crazy. I know you ain't evil. I don't know how it is that you see and hear the things you do, but I know them to be true things. So as far as I'm concerned, you ain't a woman who talks to dead people, you're just a woman. A woman I'm mighty interested in getting to know a lot better, and I don't give a good goddamn who in this town thinks they've got something to say about that."

"That might be just about the sweetest thing anybody's ever said to me, Willis." I meant it, too. Growing up the freak of a small town made for a lonely life, at least among other warm bodies. "I'm pretty interested in getting to know you a lot better, too. But not at the cost of your job." I pushed back from the table and took my glass into the kitchen and set it in the sink.

"Now you been over here way too long for any reasonable lunch break, so why don't I wash these dishes while you get on back to the station and try to catch some bad guys?"

He stood up and walked over to stand behind me, close, his breath tickling the little hairs on the back of my neck. "I'll go back to the station," he said, his voice low and husky. "But when I get off at six, I'm coming right back over here, and we're going to explore that whole 'getting to know each other better' idea."

"I'll have pork chops and mashed potatoes ready by six-thirty," I said, looking down at the sink. I didn't trust myself to turn around, or I was liable to jump him right there on my poor kitchen table.

"Keep talking sexy like that and I'll never leave," he said with a laugh. Then he put his arms around me from behind and kissed the side of my neck. "I'll see you later, Lila Grace."

I braced myself on the sink against a sudden rush of weakness in my knees. "See you soon, Willis."

I didn't turn and watch him go. I didn't even sneak a glance out of the corner of my eye at his firm butt in his uniform khakis. And I most certainly didn't sit down in my chair at the table, downing a whole 'nother glass of tea while fanning myself vigorously with the latest issue of *Southern Living*. Really, I didn't.

CHAPTER 24

"I'm in the dining room!" I called out in response the knock on the front door. "Shit," I muttered, looking at my watch. It was half past six, so that must be Willis. Sure enough, his broad shoulders filled the space in my doorway almost to the point of blotting out the last rays of late afternoon sun right about the same time I realized what time it was. He was grinning like a high school boy that just got his first car, but his smile melted when he got a good look at me and the mess I was in the middle of.

Pork chops and mashed potatoes were not steaming on the table, that's for damn sure. The only things on my dining room table were manila folders and crime scene photos, and they were spread out all over the place like a paperwork grenade went off in my house.

"I'm sorry," I said. "I really thought I'd have dinner ready, but I got to looking through all this stuff, and then Jenny and Sheriff Johnny came and started going over it all with me..." I waved a hand at where Jenny sat at the other end of the table, Johnny by her side. They looked up from the coroner's report they were poring over, waved absently like they thought Willis could see them, then went back to the paper. I didn't know what they thought was so interesting in that report, we'd read it three times.

"Don't worry about it," Willis said, years of marriage almost making him good enough to hide his disappointment. Almost. Oh well, if he had wanted to go out with a normal girl, he wouldn't have come over for lunch with the town psychic crackpot. He sat down at the nearest chair and glanced over the mess. "What have we got?"

"Nothing," I said. "And not just the normal 'I don't know what's going on here' nothing. According to Johnny, these photos look like the scene was scrubbed by somebody who knows what they're doing." I pointed to three photos that Johnny had picked out for me. "Look here. There should be footprints here if the killer broke into Jenny's house by the basement window, like y'all think he did."

The photo showed the exterior area of the Miller home. A basement window was nestled in the wall a few inches above ground level, and I knew from looking at the other pictures that the window wasn't locked. Jenny said she didn't know anything about whether or not it was usually open, because she ever went down into the basement. So it could have been left open for days or more. In front of the window was a small strip of bare dirt, then a small fifteen-by-forty vegetable garden that Mrs. Miller kept to have some fresh tomatoes, green beans, squash, and one watermelon plant that overproduced so much the poor woman had to put a folding table up in their yard loaded down with watermelon sporting a sign that said, "FREE - Take One! Please!"

In any kind of normal world, there would have been footprints or at least some kind of trace of the killer's passing left either in the dirt right in front of the window, or in the garden itself. But there was nothing. No rain fell in the few days between Jenny's death and the realization that she hadn't actually had a fatal accident, so that wasn't to blame. There was no other way to get to the window, unless Spider-Man was the murderer, and I hadn't heard of anyone named Peter Parker having a grudge against the Miller family.

"Somebody knew what they were doing," Willis said, looking at the pictures. "I thought of that."

"You did?" I asked. "Why didn't you say anything to me?"

"Mostly because I wanted to see if you came to the same conclusion," he admitted. "I don't like what this implies."

"I don't understand," I said. I didn't, either. I thought any way of narrowing the suspect pool from everyone who ever came in contact with Jenny or happened to be passing through town that night would be positive progress.

"It makes me think that someone with law enforcement experience of some sort may be the killer," Willis said.

"Well, isn't that good?" I asked. I was still confused. There couldn't be that many people with law enforcement experience... "Oh," I said.

"You got there, didn't you?"

"I see why you don't want it to be anyone in law enforcement."

"Not only do I not want to think that a man that has carried the badge could murder two high school girls in cold blood, I certainly don't want to think that it might be somebody I know and trust."

"Well," I said, not wanting to say what we were both thinking. "I reckon that means we need to see who all in town has worked security on jobs in the past or maybe served as an MP sometime."

Willis let out a breath, relief flooding his face. "Yeah, that's good. That's a good idea. I can call the local Army Reserves and National Guard units. They'll have records of any former or active-duty personnel with law enforcement training."

"I'll touch base with my second cousin Janice over at the Marine recruiting station. She can get me the information on Navy and Marines." Willis stood up, and I reached out to grab his arm. He turned and looked down at me.

I stood up, very close to him. I could smell the very lightest hints of his cologne, still clinging to his shirt collar after hours of work. "Later," I said, my lips almost grazing his chin. I let my breath carry across his neck and smiled at the shiver he gave.

"But..." His protest was a token, and we both knew it.

"Later," I said, more firmly. I poked him in the chest and pushed him back a step. "Now get out of my way, Sheriff. I promised a good-looking man pork chops for supper, and at my age, you do not want to disappoint the most eligible bachelor to move into the county in thirty years."

I stepped past him, dodging his oncoming kiss, and ducked into the kitchen to start mixing up the flour for the pork chops.

~

"You've known him a long time. Do you think Jeff could do something like this?" Willis asked, pushing back from the table, a pair of decimated pork chop bones all that remained of a helping plate of home-cooked food.

I thought about my answer for long seconds before I let out a sigh. "I don't know. If I'm being honest, I'd have to say I can't think of anybody in town that I would think could kill two little girls like that. But I wouldn't have thought that Jerry Westmoreland would run a still in the woods behind his house until his sister died and told me all about it. I wouldn't have thought that Alexander Lee Evans would have driven drunk and totaled his mama's car, then blamed it on a random car thief, but that's what he told me happened. So I reckon you just can't ever tell with people."

"I don't think he's good for these murders, but we'll have to take a real good look at him. I know he was working the football game the night Jenny was killed because he works every home game."

"That doesn't really do anything to clear him," I said. "By the time Jenny got home, Jeff would have had plenty of time to direct traffic out of the school parking lot and get over to her house."

"Yeah, it's not like it's a long drive. He wouldn't even have to speed."

"Or worry about being seen if he was in his patrol car. It's totally normal for the local boys to be running around town arresting speeders or breaking up parties and fights after home games. He could have parked right in front of the Miller house and no one would even notice."

"Or think to mention it when we interviewed the neighbors," Willis growled. "I'm having a hard time with this, Lila Grace, I gotta admit. I know I'm new here, but Jeff doesn't seem like the type to hurt anybody. I had my concerns about his ability to use his sidearm when I took over the office."

"I know, Willis, I know. He's a gentle soul. I'll agree with you there. I was surprised when he decided to go to work for Sheriff Johnny in the first place. He never showed any inclination toward law enforcement when he was little."

"How old was he when you taught him?" he asked.

"I taught Jeff in Sunday School from fourth grade all the way through high school, off and on. I floated back and forth among the grades as other teachers came and went. Since I'd been doing it forever, I just filled in for a year or two wherever there was a need. And I reckon I taught him in Vacation Bible School for almost that long. Most of the kids stop going to Bible School when they get to high school, but Jeff stayed involved with the church youth programs right up until he joined the Sheriff's Department."

Willis sat back, looking up at the ceiling light like he hoped there was some kind of answer written there. I could have told him there wasn't nothing in that ceiling light but a couple of dead mosquitoes and some spiderwebs I hadn't got around to cleaning, but I let it go. If he wanted to use my shortcomings as a housekeeper to inspire his deductions, so be it.

"Who else?" he asked, not taking his eyes off the ceiling.

"Who else what?" I replied, not having a single idea what he was asking. Sometimes I wonder how men communicate with each other, since they always want to try to use two words to ask a ten-word question. When they're alone with one another, do they just grunt and scratch themselves? I don't really want to know, I reckon.

"Who else has any military or law enforcement experience in town?"

"Oh good Lord, Willis, you might have to narrow it down a little more than that. There ain't a whole lot of people who've been police, but just about every grown man in town has served at least one tour in the service, one branch or another. And everybody here can shoot, and drive, and has watched way more *CSI* and *Law & Order* than is healthy."

"I know that, Lila Grace," he snapped, then took a deep breath. "I'm sorry. I just want to make sure we're not missing anybody. Who has recent military experience and might have been in school with the girls? If there's somebody that graduated when they were freshmen, he could have gone off to serve and come back recently."

"Well, Josh Massey just got back from Afghanistan a few months ago, and he's just about twenty-one, so he would have known the girls in school, but he didn't do this."

"How can you be sure?" Willis asked.

"He left a foot back in Afghanistan and is still learning to walk again. He won't get his first prosthetic for another month or two," I said.

"Yep, he's out. Anybody else?"

"Leonard Furting enlisted right out of high school, and there was some talk that it was because he got Barbara Harding pregnant. She never had a baby, though, and Leonard's been walking around with Jennifer Campbell ever since he got home. I don't think he knew Jenny or Shelly, but I'm not sure."

"Well, we'll look into him. Anybody else?"

"I can't think of anybody else right off the top of my head. I mean, there's Gerald Bankhead, he was the deputy before Jeff, but he's better than seventy now. Gerald's son Erskine grew up around the department and the station, but he's over three hundred pounds and walks with a limp. He ain't any more likely to sneak up on Jenny in her basement than he is to run a marathon."

Willis chuckled and got up from the table. He started clearing the table, and I stood to help. He motioned me to sit. "No, ma'am. You cooked, I clean. You just remind me where the trash can is and I'll throw these scraps out."

"Just pitch those out the back door," I said. "Professor Snape will take care of them."

"Professor Snape?" He turned to look at me. "Does the ghost of Alan Rickman haunt your garbage?"

I laughed out loud, throwing my head back and about falling out of my chair. "Oh sweet Jesus, Willis Dunleavy, you are a wonder! No, Professor Snape is what I've taken to calling this fat raccoon that prowls my backyard at night. If I toss him the scraps from my dinner, he doesn't go rummaging around in my garbage can. And he keeps the snakes away."

"Why Professor Snape?"

"I was watching the first Harry Potter movie when he appeared in my window one night. Scared the fire out of me, just in a scene where Snape was yelling at Harry about something. So I called him Professor Snape. Sometimes if we're getting along particularly well, I call him Severus."

"You are a strange, strange woman, Lila Grace Carter," Willis said. "She talks to ghosts and names wild raccoons."

"Don't forget seduces police officers," I teased.

"I haven't forgotten," he said, and the smoldering gaze he turned on me said he might not be teasing.

CHAPTER 25

Willis left a little while after he finished the dishes. We kissed on the couch for a bit, but things didn't move any further than that. I felt like it wasn't right to sleep with a man while we were trying to catch a murderer together, and to be honest, I was a little nervous. It had been quite a while since I'd lain with a man, and I wasn't sure how fast was too fast, or too slow, or what I wanted out of things with Sheriff Willis Dunleavy. I knew I liked him, I enjoyed his company, and having a man who knew how clean up after himself was certainly welcome. I just didn't know how serious I wanted to be, how serious I was prepared to be.

So I did what I always do when I'm all mixed up in my head about things; I went for a walk. I only ever end up one place. I go there so often it's almost like there's a path leading from my front door to the entrance. I ended up at the cemetery beside Woodbridge Presbyterian Church again, walking through the rows of stones with familiar names, lost in my thoughts.

I ended up sitting on a headstone marked "Good," with two names etched in it, many years apart. There was a smaller stone set into the ground beside it, marked for Tina Good, Daughter, aged eight years when she passed. It had been many years since I'd seen my old friend

Tina, but I talked to her often. This was one of the few times I felt normal, when I could go to a cemetery and not expect anyone to talk back to me. I'd watched Tina cross over with her mama, all those years ago, and she was looking down on me from a better place, just like so many people say about their deceased relatives. Unlike those people, I knew my friend wasn't still there, so I could tell her anything and not worry about getting an answer.

But I couldn't avoid the dead. Even in the far corner of the cemetery, they found me. The Dead Old Ladies' Detective Agency, as they'd taken to calling themselves, gathered around me about twenty minutes after I started my visit with Tina.

"What do we know new, Lila Grace?" Miss Faye's voice was sharp, like her piercing blue eyes, and quick, the way she had moved in life. She was all spiky energy and short, intense bursts of conversation.

"I don't know much, Miss Faye," I replied. "We're pretty sure the killer knows something about police work, or maybe was in the military. He could have been an MP, I guess."

"What makes you say that?" Miss Helen's slow drawl always reminded me of a sweet old milk cow, never in a hurry about anything, just taking the world in. Her slow speech masked a sharp mind, though. She said less than the other women, but missed nothing, and it was always best to listen when she talked.

"He didn't leave any tracks or forensic evidence, even at Jenny's house. That murder was staged to look like an accident. If there's any crime scene that would naturally be sloppy, that's the one. But he took just as much care to cover his tracks there as with Shelly's murder."

"Then have you brought him in yet?" Miss Frances asked. She stood with her arms crossed. "I'm assuming not, since you're here, but why not?" Miss Frances was a force to be reckoned with, even in death.

"We don't have any evidence that Jeff did it," I said.

"Well, not until you bring him in and he confesses," Miss Frances said. "A few hours in the back of that police station with a rubber hose and he'll sing like a canary."

"You'll have to excuse Frances," Miss Helen said. "She likes to snoop in Julia McKnight's old house and watch the old movies through the window. They've been playing a lot of old police movies this week."

"We can't beat a confession out of him," I said. "What if he's innocent? He's a respected member of the community and a police officer. He has no reason to hurt those girls."

"Not those girls, no," Miss Faye agreed. "But he sure did have a reason to wish ill on Jenny Miller's mama."

"What about my mother?" Jenny asked, appearing beside me. Most ghosts can't just pop from place to place, but Jenny was a strong spirit, with some extraordinary ability.

"I'm sorry, sweetheart," Miss Faye said, demurring. "I shouldn't speak ill of the living."

"It's not speaking ill if it helps us catch a murderer," I said. "If you know some connection between Jeff and Jenny's mother, you need to tell us."

"Now don't get feisty, young lady," the fiery ghost shot back. "Just because you're still up and walking around visible, doesn't mean you can smart off to your elders."

I took a deep breath. She was right in one sense. I couldn't force them to do anything, so I needed to keep the ghosts happy. "I'm sorry. You're right, I was rude. Was there something you wanted to tell us about Jeff and Jenny's mom? Were they connected somehow?"

"You didn't know Tara Withrow when she was little, did you? Of course not, the Baptists don't mingle too much, so you wouldn't have taught her in Vacation Bible School. Well, she was a gorgeous child, grew up a little bit wild and a little bit too fast, if you know what I mean." She made a gesture in front of her chest to indicate breasts, just in case I had even the slightest chance of missing her meaning.

She went on. "Well, Tara was a very pretty girl, and very popular, and she was always with the other popular boys and girls. The cheerleaders, the football players, the student council president, all of those things. Jeff...Jeff ran in a different circle, let's say. He wasn't the most popular boy in school, and he wasn't quite smart enough to be useful to the popular kids, so he got a lot of teasing."

"How do you know all this?" Jenny asked.

"Oh, honey, I was the secretary of the high school for thirty years. There was nothing that happened under that roof that I didn't know about." I knew from personal experience that between her and her two cohorts, their knowledge extended far past the schoolhouse walls, too.

"Senior year, Tara and some of her best girlfriends played a cruel prank on poor Jeff. He followed that child around for years like a puppy, mooning after her, carrying her books, giving her rides places when whatever boyfriend she was dating either got tired of carting her around or had something else to do, all sorts of stuff. I'm sorry, honey, but your mama was not the sweetest person when she was a teenager."

"Good lord, Faye, who is? I seem to recall you beating up half the boy's baseball team in ninth grade because they told you to join the softball team with the other girls," Miss Helen's drawl cut across the night.

Faye grinned at her, a fierce, wolfish thing. "I had a better fastball than that Bolin boy ever dreamed of having, and a strike zone too small for any of them to hit. They should have let me play, and they could have been state champions."

I cleared my throat, and Miss Faye's attention snapped back to the story. "Anyway, Tara and Alan Gilfillan had just broke up for what she swore was the last time, on account of him getting drunk down at the dam and making out with my cousin Winifred on a picnic table. I loved her, but Winnie was a pure-T slut when she was young. So Tara was single around March, and it was prom season. All the senior girls were buying dresses, and making plans, and here was Tara, queen bee of the cheerleading squad, without a date. So she gets a bright idea to soak poor old Jeff for a night on the town with all her friends."

"Now, hold on a minute," Jenny said. "How do you know that's what she was thinking? Maybe she just felt bad for him and wanted to give him a night where he felt good about himself."

Faye looked at her, and I could feel the "oh, honey" in her eyes before she opened her mouth. "Oh, honey," she said. I knew it was coming. "Oh, honey" is almost as ubiquitous as "bless your heart" as a synonym for "you poor, ignorant bastard" in the South. It's not quite as insulting. But close. "Didn't I say there wasn't nothing going on in that high school I didn't know about? Two of the other cheerleaders, I don't remember both their names, but Ellen Nance was one of them, well they were office monitors sixth period that spring, and I would hear them talk about everything under the sun. And that included what Tara was doing to Jeff."

"Now, I ain't saying that the boy didn't get something out of it, too. Not like that, Lila Grace, don't look at me like that. Tara wasn't that kind of girl. But it did Jeff a world of good to be seen going to the movies with the popular kids and to have it known all over school that he was going to the prom with the prettiest girl in the county."

Jenny beamed a little at hearing how pretty her mother was in her youth. Maybe in some way that balanced out hearing that she was a royal bitch as a teenager, in some odd kind of mental ledger than only teenage girls understand.

"So prom night came, and Jeff and Tara went out to dinner in Rock Hill with all of Tara's friends, and there was a limo, and there were group pictures, and she looked beautiful in her dress, and Jeff cleaned up pretty well in his tuxedo and matching vest. I'd say he was down-right dapper."

"I sense a 'but' coming," I said.

"Oh, darling, do you ever," Miss Faye confirmed. "Things started to go sideways once they actually got to the prom. As long as they were still in the dinner and limo part of the night, Tara kept on being nice to Jeff, and all her friends followed her lead. But when they got to the school, everything changed. I was chaperoning that year, like I did a lot of years, to keep the punch unspiked, not that people even really did that except in movies. But I liked to put on pretty dresses and see all the girls all dressed up, so I usually volunteered.

"Well, the gym was decorated like an undersea fantasy, in a *Little Mermaid* theme. There were blue lights everywhere, and ripple effects casting waves on the walls, and blue and green streamers stretched all over the gym making a canopy and hiding the rafters and basketball goals. There was a huge castle that everybody walked through to get into the dance, and tables all around. Tara and her girls walked in and went straight over to a table, which had just enough chairs so that Jeff was left standing behind her, without a place to sit.

"Then they all went to the bathroom, and Jeff was left with the football players who were dating all of Tara's friends. They all did just a fine job of making it clear Jeff wasn't welcome with them, either. Tara and her friends came back, and they all started dancing, except for Jeff, who got pushed to the side as football player after football player stepped in and danced with his date while he stood behind her chair, watching. Every time he moved toward her, she stepped away to another boy, leaving him watching just like he'd done for years.

"The last straw for Jeff was when Alan showed up and Tara danced with him for about a half hour straight, kissing him on the dance floor and all but making out in front of the whole school. Jeff finally stepped up and tried to cut in, but Alan just laughed at him. Jeff tapped him on the shoulder again, and this time Alan shoved him. Jeff stumbled back and fell, and everything on the dance floor just stopped. Every student turned and looked at Jeff, sitting on his butt in the middle of the gym, looking up at his date hanging on the arm of her ex-boyfriend, looking down at him without even an ounce of remorse in her eyes."

"She looked at Jeff sitting there for a minute, then pulled Gene back to her, kissed him right on the mouth, and went back to dancing. Jeff eventually got up and left the gym. I heard later from a friend of his that he walked all the way home, five miles in rented patent leather shoes along the side of the road, with prom-goers and class-mates driving by the whole time."

Faye gave Jenny a gentle look. "I know she's your mama, sweetie, but when she was seventeen, she was a bona fide bitch. What she did to that boy was enough to break a grown man, much less a boy. Jeff never came back to school. His grades were good enough that he could lay out the rest of the school year and still pass, so he did. He didn't show up for graduation, either. Just got his diploma in the mail. I didn't see him for several years after that, until he came home about ten years ago and took a job at the sheriff's department when his mama got sick."

"God rest her," Miss Frances said.

"What happened to Mrs. Mitchum?" I asked.

"She got breast cancer about ten years ago, and Jeff came back to be with her. It went into remission for a long time, but it came back on her last year, and by the time they caught it, it had spread to her lymph nodes. She died about a month ago," Miss Frances replied.

"Just a couple weeks before Jenny was killed," I said.

"And just a few days before Shelly reminded him of the worst night of his life," Jenny said.

I spun to look at her. "What do you mean?" I asked.

"Shelly asked him to go to prom with her," she said. "I didn't think anything of it at the time, she was always picking at people. But it was at one of the home football games, and Shelly was messing with Jeff after the game, and she asked him to go to prom with her." Her hands flew to her mouth. "Oh my god."

"What is it, honey?" I asked.

"She said we'd both go with him. Shelly told Jeff that we both wanted to date him. She set him off. Shelly got us both killed."

I stared at the girl, who leaned against a headstone, shaking her head. Just then, a patrol car with lights flashing sped by the cemetery and pulled up in front of my house. I watched Willis jump out of the car and run up my steps. As he banged on the door, I pulled out my cell phone and dialed his number. I watched him pull his phone out of his pocket and look at the screen, then put the phone to his ear.

"I'm not home, Willis. I'm at the cemetery. I'm walking your way. What's going on?" I put my feet in motion so my actions would match my words.

"Is Jenny with you?" he asked.

"Yes, and we've got some information about Jeff that you need to hear."

"Bring her with you. We've got to go."

"Go where?" I asked.

"The Miller house. I just got a call from Jenny's father. Someone kidnapped Mrs. Miller. Jenny's mother is missing."

CHAPTER 26

I explained Tara Miller's history with Jeff as we sped over to the Miller home. When I added the details of Shelly teasing Jeff, Willis shook his head. "Stupid kids," he muttered. "Messed with the wrong man, and now they ended up dead because of it."

Jenny was frantic in the back seat, flitting in and out of the car and cursing her friend Shelly with every breath. "I knew she was being a bitch, but I didn't do anything to stop her. Dammit, Shelly, why did you have to mess with his dumb ass?"

I didn't bother trying to point out the beam in her eye while she fussed about Shelly, because this wasn't the time to tell the poor dead child that she was as much to blame for her situation as Shelly. And honestly, neither one of them was much to blame. Sure, they didn't need to torment poor Jeff, but that still didn't give him cause to go murdering people, neither.

We pulled up in front of Jenny's house less than ten minutes after Willis first banged on my door. It ain't like it's that big a town, after all. Reverend Turner was sitting on the front porch, a Bible in one hand and a flashlight in the other. There was a pump shotgun leaning against the wall behind him, and I wouldn't put it much past the good

Reverend to turn that scattergun on anybody he thought to be intruding on the Millers' hour of grief.

"Reverend," Willis said as we approached the bottom step.

"Sheriff," Reverend Turner said, standing up and setting his Bible down in the seat of the rocker he'd vacated. "Lila Grace." He nodded to me. It was the most polite greeting he'd given me in better than ten years. I reckon our little heart-to-heart the other night had some effect.

"Reverend Turner," I said. "I'm sure Mr. Miller appreciates you being here for him."

The preacher looked a little ashamed but gave me what passed for an appreciative nod. "David isn't a regular member of our congregation, but Tara is one of the leaders of the church. I felt that if there was anything I could do, I should be here."

"Daddy always says he has an important meeting every Sunday morning, at the intersection of Pillow Street and Blanket Avenue," Jenny said. "But it means a lot that Reverend Turner would come out in the middle of the night like this."

I reached out and patted the man's shoulder. To his credit, he barely flinched at my unclean touch. Maybe he really was thawing toward me a little bit. Or maybe he was just too sleepy to fight. "I'm sure he appreciates it, even if he don't say it, Reverend," I said, moving past him into the house.

The Union County Sheriff's Department ain't exactly what you would call bustling, and there ain't a whole lot of manpower allocated to Lockhart most nights. So it wasn't a big surprise that there were only two people in the house when we stepped in. I recognized Larry Tolins, the night shift man in the speed trap down on Highway 49, and a reedy little fellow who ducked into the kitchen as soon as the sheriff walked in, but I was pretty sure I recognized the flaming red hair that couldn't be anybody but Chuck Blackwell. Chuck was a good man, but lazy as the day is long. I knew if he was in that kitchen, it was because it was far from any possible crime scene and close to any casseroles the grieving family might have left out on the counter.

"Larry, what do we know?" Willis asked.

"Not much, Sheriff," the dark-haired man answered. "The call came in about half an hour ago, and I called for backup as soon as I got here and saw David had been hit upside the head. Told Ava to call up everybody she could find, but Chuck was the only one who picked up the radio."

"What about Jeff?" I asked. Willis shot me a sharp look, but it was the only real question we were interested in, especially after my talk with the grapevine ghosts earlier.

"Ava said he had him a long weekend, talked about getting out of town. She didn't even bother trying to reach him. Said when he went off the grid, he went whole hog about it. No radio, no cell phone—nothing. I reckon we won't see him until Tuesday morning."

I thought there was a good chance I'd see Jeff before that, but I didn't want to say anything to Larry about it. "What does Mr. Miller say happened?" I asked.

"Not much, Ms. Carter. I talked to him, but he don't know a whole lot." He nodded at the despondent man on the sofa by the big picture window in the den.

I walked over to where David Miller sat on the couch, his elbows on his knees. He was hunched over, a man curling in on himself to keep the world out. The past week had been enough to break most people, and now his wife going missing on top of his daughter's death had him wearing the haunted expression of a man who didn't know if he had anything left to live for.

I didn't wait for Willis to give me the okay; I just sat down on the couch next to Mr. Miller. I put one arm around his shoulders and pulled him tight to me. He was a grown man, not used to having somebody able to give him comfort, but I'm an old woman, and in a small town in the South, that means I'm halfway to being everybody's aunt. I'm not bound by the laws of normal manners. Besides, everybody already thinks I'm crazy, so I get to do anything I want.

"I'm so sorry you've got to go through this, Mr. Miller. We're here, and we're going to figure out what happened, and bring your Tara back to you. I promise," I said. I saw Willis and Larry both stiffen and look at one another when I said that. I know, you ain't supposed to promise somebody something you don't know you can deliver, but I'm not a cop. I'm an old woman who hates to see people hurting, so I did what I could to help the man with his pain.

He shook in my arms for a minute, then I heard him take a long breath. I felt his shoulders tighten, so I relaxed my hold on him, and he sat up.

"Thank you, Lila Grace," he said. "I appreciate it. I know you can't really promise that, but it means a lot anyway."

"Well, I promise to try my damnedest, how about that?" I said.

"I'll take it," he replied. "Now what do I need to do to find Tara?"

Willis stepped forward. "I know you've already gone over this with Officer Tolins, but why don't you fill me in a little bit on what happened tonight, just so I can hear it fresh?" He sat down on the coffee table, positioning himself directly in front of Mr. Miller. I knew full well this didn't have a damn thing to do with him hearing anything fresh, and everything to do with making sure the man's story stayed straight. I was sure that Jeff took Jenny's mom, and I'm pretty sure that Willis was, too.

But I knew full well that the first suspect in any case was the husband, so it made sense to look at Mr. Miller while we got all our information together to go after Jeff. Besides, there might be something new that came out of his story, something he left out when he talked to Tolins.

I stood just out of Mr. Miller's line of sight, but still in the room. I didn't have any real business being there, but since the sheriff led me in, nobody else was going to have the guts to throw me out. Jenny's dad had an ice pack wrapped in a dishtowel pressed up against the back of his head, and a bruise blossoming on his cheekbone just under his right eye. Whatever happened, it wasn't pretty.

"I heard a noise," he started. "I was upstairs asleep, and something woke me. I don't know what it sounded like, just that it woke me up. I laid there in the bed for a minute, listening to see if I could hear what it was, thinking maybe it was Jenny going down for a glass of water. Then I remembered...well, then I remembered, and I got up, moving as quiet as I could manage without turning a light on."

"It sounded like somebody was trying to move through the house being real quiet, but they didn't know where all the furniture was. Hell, with all the people that have been in and out of here the last week, I barely know where the chairs are supposed to go. So I heard another sound, like somebody walking into a chair and it scraping across the floor, and heard somebody cuss real quiet, like they couldn't help it."

"What did the voice sound like?" Willis asked, leaning forward. He was all cop now, attention focused like a laser.

"I don't know," Mr. Miller said, rubbing his bruised face. "It sounded like a man, but that's all I can really remember."

"Okay, that's fine, David, just tell me everything you can remember," Willis said, reaching out and patting the distraught man on the knee.

"I looked around the bedroom, but there was nothing there I could use as a weapon, really. We don't keep guns...I mean, there's a shotgun, but it's over the fireplace, and I don't know if it'll even shoot. It was my granddaddy's. I've never even shot the thing. So I kinda snuck downstairs as quiet as I could, and when I got to the landing, there was a man coming up at me."

"He must have been as surprised as I was, but he reacted faster. The dude charged up a couple of steps and slammed me into the wall. My head cracked into the drywall behind me, and I saw stars. Then I felt something heavy hit me in the face, and I fell down. I got hit on the back of the head, and I passed out. He took me out in just a few seconds. I was useless." He put his face in his hands, and I saw his shoulders shake with sobs.

"Mr. Miller, I'm sure there's nothing more you could've done," Willis said. "But I need you to think for me, David. Do you remember any details about the man's clothes? His shoes, his pants, his face?"

"He wore a mask. One of those ski masks, with one big hole cut out for the eyes. His shirt was dark. I didn't notice really anything about it."

"Okay," Willis prodded. "What about his pants? When you fell to the ground, did you notice anything about his shoes?"

"His shoes...he wore boots, like work boots, but black. Blue jeans, I think, maybe blue work pants...I don't know. Black socks, I guess. They didn't stand out. I'm sorry, I can't...my head really hurts." A tear rolled down his face as he clutched his skull.

I looked around and saw Peggy Barnette standing in the doorway. Peggy was one of the local EMTs, a stout woman who was every bit as capable of driving the ambulance and manhandling an unconscious adult as she was putting a bandage on a child's skinned knee. I raised an eyebrow at Peggy, and she came over. Sheriff Dunleavy backed up so she could examine the man.

"Mr. Miller, I need to check your eyes." Peggy knelt in front of the distraught man and pulled a small flashlight from her shirt pocket. She flicked it across his face, and he jerked back. She turned to us. "I think he may have a concussion. His memory might be a little foggy, and he needs to go to the hospital and get checked out."

"And I need to find out everything I can about his missing wife," Willis snapped. Peggy scowled at him, but didn't reply.

I tugged on the sheriff's elbow and pulled him up with me. "We might as well go upstairs and see if there's anything up there," I said. "He won't be able to tell us anything useful—he's too upset."

Willis sighed and ran a hand through his hair. "I know. It's frustrating, is all." He waved Larry over. "Deputy Tolins, accompany Mr. Miller to the hospital. Sit by his bed in case he remembers anything. If he thinks of anything, no matter how small, you call me. Understand?"

"Yes, sir," Larry said. He walked over to where Peggy was examining Jenny's dad and bent down to speak to her.

Willis headed up the stairs, and I followed close behind. There were pictures all along the wall going up the stairs, smiling family photos from Christmas, Disneyland, a couple from when Mrs. Miller was pregnant with Jenny. We got to the top of the stairs, and I stopped, looking at Jenny. She hovered just outside the door to her parents' bedroom, as if she was afraid to set foot in the room.

"What's wrong, sweetie?" I spoke softly, so the folks downstairs wouldn't hear me.

"I...I'm scared, Miss Lila Grace. I haven't been scared this whole time, even though I've been dead. I guess it's like there's nothing left to be afraid of now. But this...she's my *mom*. I don't know what's happening to her. I just know that *he* has her, and he hates her, and..." She turned away from me, her face in her hands. I reached out to her, but my hand passed right through her shadowy form.

"I'm sorry, honey," I said. "I wish there was something I could do."

She spun back to me, a fury on her face, and I could almost feel the anger rolling off of her. The pictures on the wall shook, and I heard a muffled *thud* from inside the bedroom as one fell off the top of a dresser. She looked at me, her eyes blazing, and said, "There is. Find her. Find my mama, and make that son of a bitch *pay*."

CHAPTER 27

Willis and I left the Miller house not long after, after Willis directed Larry to take Jenny's dad to the hospital and left Chuck at the house in case any calls came in about ransom or anything else. We didn't expect the phone to ring; we both knew exactly what was going on here. I sat in the passenger seat of the sheriff's patrol car while he got on the radio and ordered dispatch to call in the auxiliary deputies. There were half a dozen or so men and women who were deputized in case of missing children or elderly folks, lost hikers, or any large-scale emergencies. Jenny rode along to the hospital with her dad, unseen and unheard, but there to see he was taken care of.

Willis opened the door and slid in behind the wheel. "Everybody will meet us here in a few minutes. I'm going to station two of them in the house, probably Stan and Clyde. They're old enough and trustworthy enough to babysit the place while Mr. Miller is getting checked out. I'll have Chuck start the canvass in one direction, and get Ernest McKnight to head down the other side of the street."

"You think that's gonna work out okay? This is still South Carolina, Willis. Some people see a black man knocking on their door in the middle of the night, they're going to answer with a twelve-gauge before they ever look to see if they know him." Ernest McKnight was a respectable businessman, one of the best mechanics I'd ever seen, and about six-and-a-half-feet tall and blacker than the ace of spades. I did not want to see that gentle giant killed by some nervous homeowner while trying to help the police.

"I'll send Irene Middleton out with him. Make sure she does the knocking, and Ernest can ask the questions. He's been an auxiliary deputy for a long time and was an MP in the army, too. He knows what kinds of things to look for."

"You know they ain't going to find anything," I said.

"I know we have to try everything we can think of," he growled.

"I'm not arguing that, Willis," I said. "I'm just saying that...well, I don't even know what I'm doing here. I can't help none with the living."

"You're helping me, Lila Grace. This is my first real case in this town, with these people. I need somebody to be my touchstone, to keep me grounded. That's why you're here—because I trust you, and because everybody here trusts you."

"Everybody here is scared shitless that I might really be able to talk to their dead relatives and find out all the dirt on them." I was grumbling, but Willis's words made me feel good, like I was useful.

"Well, there's probably a little of that, too," he agreed, and I slapped him on the arm. We both laughed, then headlights appeared, and he was out of the car to give instruction to the new arrivals.

I waited patiently for about three seconds, then started to fidget. I got out of the car, knowing full well that if I sat there much longer, I was going to start messing with the switches and buttons on the dash. The last thing any of us needed was me firing up the siren on Maple Lane in the middle of the night. Not that anybody within a mile of us was asleep. If there's one sure way to wake up small-town folk in the middle of the night, it's turn on some police lights.

I felt a chill on my arm and looked to my left, starting a little as Sheriff Johnny looked at me, his hand on my shoulder and a worried expression on his face. "Good Lord, Johnny, you scared the fire out of me!" I said. "What's wrong? I mean, more than what I already know about, that is."

Johnny didn't speak. Johnny never spoke, except for that one time a couple days ago. He was a quiet man in life, and death hadn't loosened his tongue any. Some ghosts are just barely different from when they were living, but some are mere shades of their former selves, no pun intended. Johnny seemed to be fading the longer he was around. I had a fleeting worry that he needed to cross over soon, or there wouldn't be anything left to pass on to the other side.

I don't know what that means, what waits for anyone after they leave our world for the next, but my faith tells me that even though some souls wander the Earth for a time after their bodies die, eventually they move on to a better place. Well, not all. Young Jeffrey was very quickly getting relegated to the list of people I wanted to see go to a much worse place.

"What is it, Johnny? Did you find something?" He nodded and motioned for me to follow him. I did, walking down the sidewalk several houses to the Terrance house. I knew that Jackie and Mike Terrance were in Michigan for a month, visiting their new grandbaby, so I wasn't sure what Johnny wanted me to see there. He stopped at the mouth of the driveway and pointed down, but, of course, I couldn't see anything. I pulled out my phone and turned on the flashlight app, shining the bright LED beam down at the ground. There, in the mud built up in the dip between their driveway and the street, was a set of fresh tire tracks. There was no reason for anyone to be at the Terrance house with them gone, and it had just rained a few days ago, so these tracks were almost certainly from tonight. Which meant they were Jeff's.

"Well, what about it, Johnny? We know he drove here. Are you telling me there's something about these tracks that Willis needs to know?" He nodded. "Alright, then. Let me text him, and we'll see what we can figure out." I took a photo of the tracks with my phone and texted it to Willis, telling him that Johnny pointed them out at the Terrance house.

"Stay there. Don't touch the tracks. Be there in 5," was the reply I got, so I went over and sat down on the retaining wall Mike Terrance built out of rocks he picked up out of the Broad River last summer. A few minutes later, Willis came walking up, his own flashlight cutting a narrow beam through the dark night.

I got up and walked over to the tire prints. "Here you go. I don't know what good this does us. We knew he drove here. It ain't like he was going to carry Mrs. Miller off over his shoulders."

"It tells us he ain't in his squad car," Willis said. "The treads don't match the department-issue tires. And these are big tires, not like the car I've seen Jeff drive around town. These are from a pickup, or an SUV. Maybe something with four-wheel drive. From that, I'd guess he had to do some off-roading to get to wherever he's holding Mrs. Miller, or at the very least, down some rough dirt roads."

Johnny was nodding so hard I thought his head would pop off. Obviously, Willis was saying what Johnny was thinking, I just couldn't figure out all the connections. I wracked my brain, trying to remember anything from Jeff's childhood about hunting cabins, or favorite spots in the woods, or...

"That's it," I said. "That's got to be where he took her."

"Where?" Willis asked.

"I'm not real sure, we should probably ask Cracker, but I seem to recall there being something about Jeff's daddy having a little piece of property over on John D. Long Lake, with a trailer or a fishing cabin, or something like that. I think his daddy called it his quiet place. Jeff talked one time in Sunday School about going with his daddy to the quiet place, and how much he liked it there."

"That sounds like the perfect place to take somebody if you don't want to be seen," Willis said.

"And it's not far from where he dumped Shelly's body. Do you think he might have..."

"I don't know." Willis interrupted me before my thoughts went too far down that path. "Her body was in the water too long to know if there was any kind of sexual assault, so don't think about that right now. Just think that if he's got some kind of deranged fantasy playing out in his head, that Mrs. Miller might still be alive."

"As long as we can find that place and get to her fast enough," I said.

"Welcome to the wonders of the internet," Willis said. "Let's get back to the car. We can look up property records online with the computer in the car."

I followed him back to the car and slid into the passenger seat. He tapped a few buttons and looked annoyed.

"Nothing under his name. I know he rents the house he lives in from Clint Maxwell, but whatever other place he's got oughta show up in the tax records."

"Maybe it's under his daddy's name still?" I half-asked, half-suggested. "Try Bud Mitchum."

He tapped the keys, then grimaced, shaking his head. "What's his mother's name?"

"Serinda. She was a Cowen before she married Bud. Try that, too."

A few more taps, more head shaking, then more tapping and more scowling. "Nothing. How does a person as transparent as Jeff keeps something like property hidden? I wouldn't think he was somebody that would think like that."

"I wouldn't think he was somebody that would kill two teenagers and kidnap a woman, either," I said.

"We don't know that he did, Lila Grace," Willis said, a cautious tone to his voice.

"Don't use that policeman tone of voice with me, Willis Dunleavy," I snapped. "You know as well as I do that boy is our best and only suspect, and if he don't have that woman in his fishing trailer, wherever the hell it is, we ain't got a snowball's chance in hell of getting her back. I looked into that man's eyes, and I promised him we would bring his wife home. He's already lost his little girl. That woman is the only thing left keeping him in this world, so if we can't do that, we might as well put a bullet in his head when we give him the news."

Willis's eyes were haunted, and he wore the face of a man who had told too many families their loved ones weren't coming home. "I know, Lila. I know."

I felt a little twinge in my chest. "Nobody calls me just Lila," I said.

"I do." Those two little words, in the middle of the night, sitting in a police car hunting down a murderer and trying to bring Tara Miller home safely, rang deep inside me. This was not a man who planned on just visiting in my life. He was part of me to stay. I took a deep breath, realizing I liked that feeling, then turned my attention back to the task at hand.

"Try Bruce Feemster," I said.

"What the hell is a Bruce Feemster?"

"That's Jeff's granddaddy. He's liable to have never switched the deed over when his pap died, just kept paying the tax bill every year. The county wouldn't care, as long as they got their little piece of money, and Jeff probably never thought anything about it."

"Well, I'll be damned," Willis muttered. "There it is. A little six-acre plot on the lake, a couple miles from the main road. Ain't no way to get there in a car, but I reckon that old Bronco of Jeff's would do just fine. It's got about fifty yards of frontage onto the lake, just enough for a little dock to fish off of."

"If he's anywhere, that's where he'll be," I said. "We ain't getting there in this Chevrolet, though. We'll take my pickup. It'll get us through about anything."

"Then let's go bring her home," Willis said, putting the car in gear and tearing off on a ghost-fueled rescue mission.

CHAPTER 28

I pulled my truck off to the side of the dirt road as soon as I saw the lights of the trailer up ahead. It looked to be about a quarter mile away yet, but my big old Bessie made enough noise that if Jeff was paying any kind of attention, he already knew we were there. Willis got out of the passenger side and made some kind of gesture to me like he expected me to wait in the car.

I hate to disappoint people, really I do. Except it seems like my whole life has been one long string of disappointments to somebody. I disappointed my daddy by not being a boy he could teach to play baseball. I disappointed my mama by not being the normal little lady she wanted to raise and marry off. I disappointed more than a few boys in high school by keeping my knees together a lot longer than they hoped, and now I was about to disappoint Sheriff Willis Dunleavy because there was no way on God's green Earth I was staying in that truck.

I opened the driver's door and got out, leaving the door hanging open behind me. The dome light in old Bessie burned out about seven or eight years ago, and I never bothered replacing it. I left the keys in the ignition in case we needed to get out of there quick, and besides, the number of grand theft auto cases in the woods of Union County are about even with the number of votes George Wallace got in Harlem when he ran for President.

"Get back in the truck," Willis hissed at me. "I am not taking a civilian into what might an active hostage scene."

"Then you should have thought about that before you let the civilian use her truck to drive you to the scene. I'm going up there. Jeff and I have always had a good relationship. I might be able to help the situation."

He glared at me, and I could see the wheels turning behind his brown eyes. I know he was weighing his chances of getting me to do what he wanted, and after a few seconds, he came to the right decision —his chances were slim and none. And Slim just left town. I relaxed a little bit when I saw that acceptance come over him, because the last thing I wanted to do was waste time and energy arguing with Willis in the middle of the woods while Jeff was a couple hundred yards away maybe hurting Jenny's mama.

"Come on, but stay behind me," he grumbled, starting back toward the house.

I nodded and reached back inside the truck for the double-barrel 12-gauge behind the seat. I was willing to go into the house, but I wasn't going in there without a little backup of my own. Just because I wasn't the son Daddy hoped for didn't mean he wasn't willing to teach me how to hunt, fish, and shoot. That old gun hadn't been fired in months, but I took it out to behind Theresa Montgomery's house a couple times a year and shot up some tin cans to make sure I still knew which end to point toward the target. I cracked the gun open to make sure it was loaded, then slung it over my shoulder and caught up to Willis.

"I thought you told me you kept the shells in the glove compartment," he said, his voice low.

"I keep the extra shells in the glove box," I said. "Out here in the country we've got a name for an unloaded shotgun."

"What's that?"

"A bat."

He snorted a little laugh, then sobered as we stepped into the clearing around the trailer. It was a single-wide that had seen better days. And better decades. It started life as white with a wide blue stripe around it, but most of that was replaced with rust. The under-pinning, if there's ever been any, was long gone, and what passed for steps was just a half dozen cinderblocks with nothing resembling a handrail. A couple of the windows were gone, and yellow lamp light shone from what I assumed was the living room. I saw a figure moving inside, waving his arms and pacing, and from where we were, it looked enough like Jeff for me to decide we were in the right place.

Jenny appeared at my elbow, rising up out of the ground with Sheriff Johnny at her side. "Dad's okay. He doesn't have a concussion, so they're sending him home. Is she in there?"

"We don't know yet," I whispered. Willis's head whipped around at my voice, and I pointed to where Jenny stood, invisible to him. He nodded, then put his finger to his lips. I nodded and fell silent.

Jenny walked up to the trailer, then through the door. It always strikes me funny, how long it takes for the dead to shake their hold on habits from life. She didn't need to go through the door, she could have walked through any wall just as easily, but the habit of years had her use the door, even if she was passing through it. I made a mental note to myself to ask Johnny about that when we finished up here. Of course, he was less than half a year dead himself, so he probably still had quite a few hangups from his time walking the earth.

Willis started forward, and I put a hand on his shoulder. I leaned down close to his ear, so there was no chance of my words traveling, and said, "Jenny's inside. She can tell us what's going on in there."

"I hope her mother is still alive," Willis said.

"Me too," I agreed. "The poor child doesn't need to see that."

Jenny returned seconds later, a worried look on her face. "She's alive. He hasn't hurt her, but he's got her tied to a chair. The place is all made up with candles and flowers, like he's trying to make it romantic. He keeps yelling at her, telling her how she ruined his life at the prom, how he couldn't help it when Shelly and me said that to him about going out with him, how he's sorry, but she's got to see how much he loves her. He's crazy. Y'all have got to get in there."

I kept my face next to Willis's and relayed everything just as it came out of Jenny's mouth. He nodded, then turned to me. "He's devolving. We don't have much time. If we don't get in there in the next couple of minutes, he's going to kill her. I'll go in the front door; you go around to the back. If he draws on me, shoot him."

"Give me thirty seconds to get back there. It's dark as the bottom of a well out here," I said. I took a deep breath, steadied my nerves, and peeled off to the right to creep around the trailer as best I could. I felt like I stepped on every branch and dry leaf in the county walking that fifty yards and froze in my tracks three times waiting on Jeff to shoot me from a window, but I made it to the back door and up the rickety cinderblocks. The knob turned under my hand, and I pulled the door open, sticking my head in a foot or so above floor level. I looked down the fake wood-paneled hallway toward the living room and saw Tara Miller's back to me. She was tied to a ladder-back wooden chair, the kind found in countless dining room sets all across the South.

I didn't see Jeff at first, but he came into my view a second later, pacing and shaking his head. He was muttering something I couldn't hear, but to be honest, all my attention was on the pistol in his hand. It was a boxy black thing that I guessed was his department-issued gun, and it looked like a handful of deadly in the light of the small lamp on the end table. Jeff's head whipped around, and he trained his gun off to his left toward something I couldn't see, then I heard Willis's voice cut through the night like the crack of a whip.

"Drop the gun, son. This has to end right now."

The second Willis spoke, I pulled the back door wide open and stepped up into the hallway. The top step wobbled as my weight shifted, and it threw me off balance. I stumbled forward and crashed into the wall. Jeff spun in my direction and fired his gun, missing my head by inches. The bullet dug into the wall behind me, and I dove onto my belly. My shotgun hit the brown shag carpet and tumbled away from me, leaving me unarmed and sprawled on my face less than twenty feet away from a murderer that I still remembered as a cherubic little boy in my Sunday School class.

I heard another shot boom through the enclosed trailer, and Jeff whirled around, firing his gun three times. There was a crash from somewhere in the living room that I couldn't see, then Jeff was back in my line of sight, standing right in front of Tara Miller with his gun aimed at her face.

He looked down the hall at me, and as I got to my feet and picked up my shotgun, he got a confused look on his face. "Ms. Carter? What are you doing here?"

"I'm here to end this, Jeff. You need to let Mrs. Miller go and put the gun down," I said, walking down the hall toward him.

He pointed the pistol at me, but I saw his hand shaking even as far away as I was. I didn't stop. "You're not going to shoot me, Jeff. You always liked me in Sunday School, and I always liked you. Now put that gun away and let's talk about this."

"I can't talk about nothing no more, Ms. Carter. I done killed the sheriff, and I killed them two girls, and now I'm going to kill this bitch here. Then I'm going to shoot myself and go to Hell for all eternity where I belong." Tears ran down his face, and rage mixed with terror at what he had done.

"Jeff, this isn't you," I said. "Tell me what happened. We can work it out. We can get you help. You—"

"There's no help for this bastard!" Tara Miller screamed from the chair. She'd been so quiet to this point I thought he had her gagged, but evidently not. "Don't you lie to him. You tell him the truth. That he needs to just blow his damn brains out and rot in Hell until the end of time for what he did to my baby girl."

"Mrs. Miller, that isn't helping," I said, trying to keep my voice calm while wanting to smack her upside the head with the butt of my shotgun. I looked over at Jenny, who shrugged as if to say, "What can I do?"

I stepped into the living room and leaned the shotgun against the wall. "There, Jeff. See? I put my gun down. Now I'm not going to hurt you, and I know you don't want to hurt me. So let's talk about this, and see what we can figure out." I looked past the distraught deputy, sweat stains soaking the armpits and neck of his uniform shirt, his normally neat brown hair disheveled, and tears streaking his cheeks.

Willis lay slumped against the far wall of the trailer, half on the threadbare carpet by the door, half on the worn linoleum of the kitchenette area. His gun was loose in his grip, and his eyes were closed. I couldn't see enough to tell if he was breathing, and the dark shirt he wore hid any signs of blood, but he didn't even move an eyelid at my voice.

"I told you, there's no helping me now, Ms. Carter," Jeff wailed. "It's just like high school, only worse! I should have never trusted her then, and I should have never spoke to her kid now. These damn women have ruined my life, and now I'm going to kill the last one, and be done with it. I'm real sorry, but since you're here, I'm going to have to kill you, too."

He raised the pistol to aim it at my face, and this time, his hand was rock steady.

CHAPTER 29

I was stuck in a ramshackle trailer in the middle of the woods in a makeshift fishing camp nobody knew about, with a crazy as a loon deputy turned murderer pointing a pistol at my head. My only living backup was shot and unconscious on the floor across the room, and I, being a genius hostage negotiator who's seen way too much *Law and Order*, had disarmed myself. So all I had to save me was my wits and a couple of ghosts.

This was not how I thought I would die, let me just be clear about this. Like everybody, I've imagined my own death on more than one occasion. When I was younger, I assumed I would die at home, surrounded by a passel of grand- and great-grandchildren, my descendants all dutifully weeping in the parlor while I passed my last breath in some lavender-scented dignity that in no way involves messing my bed or any other bodily fluids.

As I grew older, and my lack of descendants became more pronounced, I realized that if I was lucky, I would be able to shuffle off my mortal coil in a decently appointed rest home somewhere, but if the cost of things continued to do what they inevitably do, I would most likely be relegated to some state-run old folks' home with last week's sheets and yesterday's Depends.

At no point did I envision myself getting shot in a trailer while trying to save a woman who despised me from a former student who once idolized me while my brand-new boyfriend lie perforated on the floor and two dead people watched the whole sideshow unfold like a tawdry hillbilly episode of *Murder, She Wrote*.

"Jeff." I switched into my "teacher voice," and his head snapped up. It was good to see I still had it, at least a little. I managed to hold my voice steady and my expression severe. "This has gotten ridiculous. Put that gun down, untie that woman, and turn yourself in immediately. You are not going to shoot me, and you are not going to hurt anyone else tonight. What Tara and her friends did to you back then was awful, but it did not ruin your life. It ruined your prom, but anything that happened after that night was your responsibility."

"I couldn't go back to school!" he wailed. "I couldn't take them laughing at me in the halls. Every time I saw somebody from school, I knew that was all they were talking about."

"For a few days, yes," I agreed. "You were a laughingstock. For a little while. But you know as well as I do that children can't keep a thought in their head longer than five minutes. You would have had a bad week, maybe two, but by the time school was out, it would have all blown over. But you didn't let it, did you?" I poured it on. I knew the only way I was walking out of that trailer was to get him to move off his plan of killing us all, and this was the only thing I could think of to do that.

"No," he said, his voice wavering. "You don't know what it's like to have everybody whisper about you."

"I don't? Boy, have you even *lived* in this town? Who do you think you're talking to? Why, the woman in that chair right there wouldn't even eat my damn chicken pot pie because Reverend Turner convinced her that Satan helped me bake it. Like the devil himself would help me dice carrots," I said with a laugh.

My voice softened, and I took a step closer. "Jeff, sweetie, I've been the one they talk about behind their hands for fifty years, and I'm still here. My front yard has had more toilet paper in the trees than the principal's house, and I've been thrown out of more Bible study groups than the Whore of Babylon. I know exactly what it's like to have the whole town staring at you, and talk about you, and that's how I know that it don't hurt. All you have to do is hold your head up and walk on by. If you don't acknowledge the fools, they can't touch you."

He looked up at me, his eyes full. "But I let them. I let them, and they just kept going, and going. That's why I didn't get the sheriff's job, because I wasn't strong enough. It's why I never got married, because I was too weak. Well, I'm not weak now! I'm strong! I'm strong, and everybody's going to know how strong I am!"

His gun, which had drifted to point toward the ground while I spoke, snapped up and pointed at Tara Miller's head from less than three feet away. There was nothing I could do, no way I could get there in time. He was going to kill that woman, and all I could do was watch.

But Jenny didn't. Jenny, sweet, dead Jenny, who helped start all this in motion by picking at Jeff with her stupid little pretty girl teasing, summoned up enough energy somehow to smack his wrist away and send the bullet slamming through the side of the trailer. Jeff looked down at his hand, then looked to where Jenny was standing right in front of him.

She looked more solid than any ghost I'd ever seen, and the way the color ran out of his face, I knew Jeff saw her, too. He staggered back, raising his gun and firing into her face three times. The bullets passed right through her, barely making the girl's image flicker, and he backed up more until he slammed into the small bar separating the kitchen and living room.

"Jenny?" Tara's voice was soft, thready, a timid little thing that might escape at any moment.

Jenny turned to her mother, and Jeff did at the same time. He raised his pistol again, but before Jenny could whirl back to strike his hand, another shot rang out, followed by two more. Jeff's eyes went wide, and his legs went rubbery as he collapsed straight down, blood pouring out onto the carpet.

I looked to Willis, who sat on the floor holding his pistol, smoke wafting from the barrel. "You're alive!" I said, thrilled and surprised in equal measure.

"This is one of those nights I'm glad I bought new vests for the department when I started. I reckon I'm also glad not everybody decided to wear them." He nodded to Jeff, who lay on the floor, his eyes open and glassy.

Before my eyes, his spirit peeled up from his body, looked around the room, and shook his head. "I'm sorry," he said. "For everything." Then he vanished, a small dark hole opening up in the air around him and taking him to wherever he was destined to spend eternity.

"Apology not accepted, asshole," Jenny replied, and my head whipped over to where she stood by her mother's chair. A bright white light appeared behind her, and she looked up at me with a wistful smile. "I guess it's time for me to go, huh?"

"Yes, sweetie, it's time for you to go," I said.

"What's happening?" Jenny's mother said, her head whipping around.

"There's a white light opening up right past that wall over there, and Jenny is supposed to go to it. She's done what she stayed here to do, and now it's time for her to go." Tara smiled at my words, but one tear slid down her cheek all the same.

"Time for me, too," came a gravelly voice from the kitchen as Sheriff Johnny walked through the bar and headed to the light. "I think my town will be in fine hands. But tell that boy to take care of my people, or he won't like it when I come back to pay him a visit."

"Will do, Sheriff," I said with a smile.

Jenny and the sheriff walked into the light, which blossomed to blinding brilliance before fading to just water-stained paneling once more. "They're gone," I said. I felt a strange wetness on my own face and reached up to find tears on my cheeks. I didn't even know I was crying, and I certainly wasn't sad, but it was a night full of emotions, that's for certain.

I helped Willis up off the floor, and we untied Mrs. Miller, then we waited outside for the ambulance and coroner and crime scene unit to arrive. I scrounged up a blanket from behind the seat of my truck to put around Tara, since she was in her pajamas, and then Willis went down to pull my truck up into the yard beside Jeff's Bronco. We told our story more times than we cared to, leaving out any mention of dead sheriffs or daughters, and the sun was peeking over the horizon before we finally pulled back onto the highway and headed back to my house.

We didn't speak as we walked in the front door; I just reached back and took his hand. I led Willis through the house to my bedroom, undressed him, and laid beside him, feeling his solid masculinity next to me as I drifted off to sleep. There would be more to come, I was sure, but there was plenty of time for that.

EPILOGUE

There were only three of us at the graveside for Jeff's funeral. Me, Willis, and Reverend Turner. The rest of the deputies disavowed any connection with the murderer, and I couldn't really blame them. The town tried its best to forget they ever knew the man, too, because to claim him would be to claim their part in making him what he was, to claim their tiny piece of guilt. His family was long dead, the only person in the world who depended on him was a sweet little Corgi named Butch, who I had on a leash next to me at the funeral.

Reverend Turner spoke kind words about the man, ignoring his end and focusing on the parts of his life he spent in service. He kept it short, though, not needing to embellish for his audience of two. When he was done, I knelt beside the casket for a moment and prayed for him. I knew full well he wasn't in a better place, I'd seen him go, but maybe my prayers could lessen his sentence a little bit. The things he did were terrible, and he deserved to pay for them, but he was, in the end, a pitiful, scared little man, and that deserved a little leniency.

Reverend Turned stepped over to me and extended his hand. "Lila Grace, I feel I may have wronged you," he said, looking me straight in the eye.

I stood up, brushed the dirt off my knees, and shook his hand. "All is forgiven, Reverend. I appreciate you speaking here today."

"If I don't minister to the lost, what kind of shepherd would I be?" he asked with a gentle smile. "I don't understand what you do, but I believe now that there is no malice in you, and no touch of evil in your gifts."

"Thank you, Reverend. I might not ever turn Baptist, but I reckon we can at least sit next to each other at the church softball games," I said, smiling back at him.

He shook hands with Willis and turned to walk into the church. Willis raised an eyebrow at me. "That was unexpected."

"Not really. We had a talk a little while ago. I think he learned a thing or two."

"Maybe you can teach an old dog new tricks," Willis said with a grin.

"Maybe," I said, grinning back. "As long as one of those tricks is putting the toilet seat down, we'll be fine."

We laughed as we walked back to the patrol car. I stopped at the door and looked back at the grave, where three filmy images of old woman wavered in the wind. The Dead Old Ladies' Detective Agency had helped solve their first case, and even if it didn't end happily for everyone, it did end, and we did put Jenny Miller to her heavenly rest. I had to count that as a win, I decided.

Then I slid into the passenger seat of the sheriff's car and let my boyfriend drive me home, the first time that had happened in my fifty-seven years. I guess that was another win, this one for the Living Old Lady.

NOTE FROM THE AUTHOR

Let's get this out of the way—none of the people in this story are real. Okay, maybe it's better to say that *all* of the people in this story are real, but not in a bad way. This version of Lockhart, which is about nine miles from where I grew up in rural South Carolina, is actually a mashup of the real Lockhart, where my dad's cousin Johnny Thomas ran the barber shop where we got our hair cut, with a healthy dose of Sharon, the town where I went to church and elementary school, and a little bit of York, all mixed in together.

The closest thing to real people in here are the Grapevine ladies. My mother, Frances Hartness, along with Faye Russell, and Helen Good were the network for all news in Western York County for decades. Mama held down the very tip of the Western triangle, with Miss Helen ("Tot") in the middle of Sharon, and Miss Faye covering the Hickory Grove end of the news. All of these women were married, but in the 70s and 80s in the rural South, you just referred to these women as "Miss First Name." It was the same as calling them "Aunt Faye" or "Aunt Helen," which I certainly would have felt perfectly natural doing. Miss Faye is the only one of the trio still around, after Miss Tot's passing last year and my mother's death two years prior, but she's still spry and sharp as a whip, as we say.

None of my family talk to dead people. Well, I was being completely sincere about one thing—all Southerners talk to dead people, and country folk more than most. So pretty much everyone in my family talks to dead people. Just for us, they don't talk back. A lot of times I wish they would.

So, this was in no way intended to mock small town Southern life. It's much more a love letter to the people who raised me, who taught me how to take care of people, how to respect people, and how to be proud of where you're from. Because I am proud of growing up a country boy. I still drive my pickup truck, call my daddy "sir," and pull over to the side of the road when a funeral procession comes along. And my tea will always be sweet, thank you very much.

So I want to thank the people that didn't even know they contributed to this book: Dr. Clyde & Nora Mitchum, Nora Jean Hope, Hazel Montgomery, Bonnie & Jean Dowdle, Faye & Margaret Hood, Bill & Lib Shillinglaw, Bo & Henny Mickle, and so many more. I appreciate the lessons they taught me. I haven't forgotten where I came from, and I never will.

ACKNOWLEDGMENTS

Thanks as always to Melissa Gilbert for all her help, and for trying in vain to teach me where the commas go.

Thanks to Natania Barron for her amazing covers, and of course to all of you for reading!

The following people help me bring this work to you by their Patreon-age. You can join them at Patreon.com/johnhartness.

Sean Fitzpatrick
Sarah J. Ashburn
Noah Sturdevant
Mark Ferber
Andy Bartalone
Nick Esslinger
Sharon Moore
Wendy Taylor
Sheelagh Semper
Charlotte Henley Babb
Wendy Kitchens
Andrew Bolyard
Darrell Grizzle

Lawrence Nash
Delia Houghland
Douglas Park Jr.
Travis & Casey Schilling
Michelle E. Botwinick
Carol Baker
Leonard Rosenthol
Lisa Hodges
Patrick Dugan
Leia Powell
Noella Handley
Butch Howard
Bob
Robin Castellanos
Lars Klander
Vickie DiSanto
Jared Pierce
Jeremy Snyder
Candice Carpenter
Theresa Glover
Salem Macknee
Trey Alexander
Brian Tate
Jim Ryan
Andrea Judy
Anthony D. Hudson
John A. McColley
Melissa Cole
Mark Wilson
Dennis Bolton
Shiloh Walker/J.C. Daniels
Andrew Torn
Sue Lambert
Emilia Agrafojo
Tracy Syrstad

Russell Ventimeglia
Elizabeth Donald
Samantha Dunaway Bryant
Sheryl R. Hayes
Bill Schlichting
Steven R. Yanacsek
Scott Furman
Rebecca Ledford
Ray Spitz

STAY IN TOUCH!

If you enjoyed this book, please leave a review on Amazon, Goodreads, or wherever you like.

If you'd like to hear more about or from the author, please join my mailing list at http://www.subscribepage.com/g8d0a9.

You can get some free short stories just for signing up, and whenever a book gets 50 reviews, the author gets a unicorn. I need another unicorn. The ones I have are getting lonely. So please leave a review and get me another unicorn!

ABOUT THE AUTHOR

John G. Hartness is a teller of tales, a righter of wrong, defender of ladies' virtues, and some people call him Maurice, for he speaks of the pompatus of love. He is also the best-selling author of EPIC-Award-winning series *The Black Knight Chronicles* from Bell Bridge Books, a comedic urban fantasy series that answers the eternal question "Why aren't there more fat vampires?" In July of 2016, John was honored with the Manly Wade Wellman Award by the NC Speculative Fiction Foundation for Best Novel by a North Carolina writer in 2015 for the first Quincy Harker novella, *Raising Hell.*

In 2016, John teamed up with a pair of other publishing industry ne'er-do-wells and founded Falstaff Books, a publishing company dedicated to pushing the boundaries of literature and entertainment.

In his copious free time John enjoys long walks on the beach, rescuing kittens from trees and getting caught in the rain. An avid *Magic: the Gathering* player, John is strong in his nerd-fu and has sometimes been referred to as "the Kevin Smith of Charlotte, NC." And not just for his girth.

Find out more about John online
www.johnhartness.com
http://www.subscribepage.com/g8d0a9

ALSO BY JOHN G. HARTNESS

FALSTAFF BOOKS

**Want to know what's new
And coming soon from
Falstaff Books?**

Try This Free Ebook Sampler

https://www.instafreebie.com/free/bsZnl

**Follow the link.
Download the file.
Transfer to your e-reader, phone, tablet, watch, computer,
whatever.
Enjoy.**